DO YOU WANT FRIES WITH THAT?

**Other Scholastic books
by Martyn Godfrey:**

Alien Wargames

The Day the Sky Exploded

The Carol & Wally Series:
  Here She is, Ms Teeny-Wonderful
  It Isn't Easy Being Ms Teeny-Wonderful
  Send in Ms Teeny-Wonderful
  Wally Stutzgummer, Super Bad Dude

The JAWS Mob Series:
  Meet You in the Sewer
  Just Call Me Boom Boom

Monsters in the School

*I Spent My Summer Vacation Kidnapped
into Space*

The Great Science Fair Disaster

*There's a Cow in my Swimming Pool
(with Frank O'Keeffe)*

MARTYN GODFREY

DO YOU WANT FRIES WITH THAT?

Cover art by
Sharif Tarabay

SCHOLASTIC CANADA LTD.
Toronto, New York, London, Sydney, Auckland

Scholastic Canada Ltd.
123 Newkirk Road, Richmond Hill, Ontario, Canada L4C 3G5

Scholastic Inc.
555 Broadway, New York, NY 10012, USA

Scholastic Australia Pty Limited
PO Box 579, Gosford, NSW 2250, Australia

Scholastic New Zealand Limited
Private Bag 94407, Greenmount, Auckland, New Zealand

Scholastic Publications Ltd.
Villiers House, Clarendon Avenue, Leamington Spa,
Warwickshire CV32 5PR, UK

Canadian Cataloguing in Publication Data

Godfrey, Martyn
  Do you want fries with that?

ISBN 0-590-24699-2

I.Title.

PS8563.034D6 1996   jC813'.54   C96-930918-X
Pz7.G63Do 1996

Copyright © 1996 by Martyn Godfrey. All rights reserved.

No part of this publication may be reproduced or stored in a retrieval
system, or transmitted in any form or by any means, electronic,
mechanical, recording, or otherwise, without written permission of the
publisher, Scholastic Canada Ltd., 123 Newkirk Road, Richmond Hill,
Ontario, Canada L4C 3G5. In the case of photocopying or other
reprographic copying, a licence must be obtained from CANCOPY
(Canadian Reprography Collective), 6 Adelaide Street East, Suite 900,
Toronto, Ontario, M5C 1H6.

 6 4 5 3 2 1   Printed in Canada   6 7 8 9/9
              Manufactured by Webcom Limited

Contents

Chapter One

Best Friends

"I don't believe this, Britt," Laura said. "This is totally exciting."

I closed my magazine and studied the cover photo for the umpteenth time. Justin Adams flashed his famous, cute, dimpled half-grin. I smiled back at him. Then I leaned closer to my best friend. "Maybe you should keep your voice down, Laura. You've been talking really loud ever since we got here. I've noticed a couple of people staring at us."

Laura checked out the passengers in the waiting room of the Toronto airport. "So what? They're just staring because we're young. I can't believe how old everybody is. We're going to be the only kids on the plane. I don't think I've seen so much gray hair and so many bald heads in one place before."

1

"Shush," I warned. "They'll hear you."

"My mom says a lot of people retire in Florida. That's probably why there are so many old people getting on the plane. But I don't really care about gray hair and bald heads. I'm too excited." Then she paused. "What am I saying? I sure say dumb stuff sometimes, don't I?"

"Yeah," I agreed. "And right now, you're saying it too loud."

"I always talk loud when I'm excited." Laura lowered her voice a little. "I've been a loudmouth since I was a little kid. Have I ever told you that?"

"I figured it out real fast when I first met you," I said.

"You don't really care how loud I'm talking, do you?" Laura went on. "I mean, you understand why I'm excited. We're going to spend spring break in Florida. We're going to the swamp."

"The Everglades," I corrected.

"And we're going to the Disney/MGM Studios at Disney World." A dopey look washed over her face. "We're going to see Justin Adams. Cute, adorable Justin Adams. I wish he was in our class. If he was, I'd like it a lot more. I'd squish in beside him in his desk and do his math for him."

I laughed.

"Why are you laughing?" Laura wanted to know.

"I'm imagining the look on Mrs. Dawson's face. Her chin would drop to her knees if she ever saw you squashed into a desk beside a boy."

"Not just any boy," she said. "Justin Adams."

"It could never happen anyway. Justin is old enough to be in eighth grade."

"Maybe he would decide to do seventh grade again because he wanted to be in my math class," Laura reasoned.

I smiled again. "You were right — you do say dumb stuff sometimes."

"I can't help it if I have an active imagination, Britt. I'm a Justin fan."

"I think you're the world's *biggest* Justin fan. I mean, you have posters of him on the ceiling in your bedroom. You have pictures of him plastered all over your locker. And you never, ever, not for any reason, miss seeing *Do You Want Fries With That?*"

Laura grinned. "You like him just as much. You're in his fan club too. I just can't wait to get to the studio so we can be part of a live audience for the best TV show in history."

I crossed my fingers. "I only hope they let us in."

"It'll be the greatest thing that has ever happened to me. Me and Justin Adams in the same room. To be able to see his dreamy blue eyes in real life. Aaah." She sighed, long and deep, slumped in her chair and pretended to faint.

"I hope it comes true, but I can't shake the feeling something will go wrong," I said. "Maybe we shouldn't get our hopes up. He might not be there. And even if he is, they might not let ordinary people like us see his show."

Laura opened her eyes and stuck her nose in the air. "Ordinary? You may be an ordinary person, but I'll have you know that I, Laura Ledington, am a very important person." She smiled and showed a mouthful of braces.

"I'm sort of looking forward to seeing the boy who plays Justin's younger brother. Little Mike Davies," I said. "He's pretty cute."

"Little Mike Davies?" Laura scoffed. "I don't think he's cute. He's all freckles and curly red hair."

"You have freckles and curly red hair," I pointed out.

She thought for a second. "I was wrong.

He's super cute. But he's only five. You can't compare five-year-old cute to Justin Adams's thirteen-year-old cute." She pretended to faint again.

"You're weird," I said.

She sat up quickly and winked at me. "I know. And you're weird too. That's why we've been best friends for so long."

* * * * *

Actually, we'd only been best friends for two months.

Only eight weeks before, Laura had walked into my seventh grade homeroom class for the first time. No, walk isn't the right word. She marched into the class, clutching a new binder stuffed with hundreds of sheets of loose-leaf paper.

Mrs. McKay, the assistant principal, shuffled in behind her. "Boys and girls," she announced, "This is Laura Ledington. She's from Vancouver and moved to Toronto on the weekend."

Laura flashed silver in the broadest grin I'd ever seen. "Hi there. Nice to meet everybody."

I liked her right away.

At lunch time, she plonked beside me at the cafeteria table. "I love your eyes," she said. "They're so round. They're perfect for your tiny nose. Your eyes twinkle. Do you know that? They twinkle and they're so brown. And your skin is so shiny. It's such a neat shade of brown. Just like the color of a horse I used to ride. His name was Chestnut. You don't mind me saying that, do you? I mean it as a compliment."

"Thanks, I guess."

"You're really pretty. Do you want to be friends? I just moved here and you look like you'd be a terrific friend. You'll like me. I'm . . . "

And she proceeded to tell me her life story. How she'd been born in Edmonton. How she'd moved around Canada a lot because her engineer parents liked living in different cities every couple of years. About her dopey sister in third grade and her bratty brother in kindergarten. About the time she'd kissed a boy at a sixth grade school dance in Vancouver and how her braces had cut his lip. And so on.

There was something about the energy radiating from her round freckled face, curly red hair and eyes so green they were almost neon, that made me open up to her immediately.

I found myself telling her about my family: that my mom was born in Cuba and escaped on an overloaded boat. How my dad, who was living in Miami, met her shortly after she learned English. They got married in Florida and then moved to Canada. How I was an only child. About the apartment I shared with my mom and my pet cat, Noda. How my parents split when I was in fourth grade. How my father moved back to Miami and worked for a big insurance company. How I visited him down south once a year. And so on.

We became instant friends.

*****

"I think we're such good friends because the same things make us laugh," Laura went on. "Do you remember when we had to cut up the worm in science class and Lucy-Mae Bennett threw up all over her binder? I laughed so hard I thought I was going to hurl too."

"Maybe we're best friends because we can act silly better than anybody else," I told her. "Like when you moved the FOR SALE sign from Mr. Pollard's house and stuck it on the front lawn of the school."

"I was planning to put the sign back that evening," she argued. "How was I supposed to guess a developer would just walk in and offer the principal some money?"

We laughed at the memory.

"How about when we accidentally tripped while we were walking past the boys' change room?" Laura continued. "And we accidentally bumped the door so it swung open and we accidentally got to see the grade eight boys' gym class getting changed?"

"Some accident. We did it on purpose. But I honestly didn't think any boys would be in there. I nearly died of embarrassment."

"The boys nearly died of embarrassment too," she noted. "But we couldn't stop laughing for the rest of the week, could we?"

"Well, we had plenty of time in detention. You know, I am really looking forward to spending a week at Disney World with you," I confessed. "We're going to have a terrific trip."

"Yeah," she agreed. "I'll bet all kinds of interesting things are going to happen."

Chapter Two

Fruit Fly Years

"All set, girls," Mom called from across the waiting room. She and an Air Canada flight attendant walked up to us.

"You bet, Mrs. Prentice," Laura said as we stood up. "I can't wait to leave cold, wet Toronto and get to that hot swamp."

Mom introduced us to the flight attendant. "This is my daughter, Brittany. And this is her best friend, Laura."

The flight attendant smiled politely. "My name is Susan. Your mother has asked me to make sure you get safely on and off the plane. I understand your father is going to meet you at the Miami airport?"

"That's where he lives," I answered.

"Britt visits her dad once a year." Laura filled in the details of my personal life for Susan. "This time he sent an extra ticket so she could bring a friend. I'm the lucky person. He's going to drive us through the swamp. Then we're going to Disney World to see Justin Adams."

"That should be lots of fun," Susan said. "But I'm afraid I don't know who Justin Adams is. Is he a relative of yours?"

"I wish," I said as I watched Laura's mouth drop. She stared stupidly at Susan, as if she couldn't believe she'd met somebody who didn't know who Justin Adams was.

"He's an actor on *Do You Want Fries With That?*" she told Susan. "You must have seen it on TV. It's a comedy that takes place in a fast-food restaurant. Everybody watches it. Justin is the boy with the long blond hair and gigantic blue eyes. He works the French fry cooker."

Mom winked at Susan. "He's a definite heart-throb," she added. "If I was twelve years old, he'd be my absolute dreamboat."

"He's not a drumbeat, Mrs. P. He's gnarly-cute," Laura said. "And I'm almost thirteen."

"Sorry," Mom apologized. "I know how much a year means to you at your age, Laura."

Laura looked puzzled. "Doesn't a year mean a lot to people at your age too, Mrs. P?

10

Brittany says you tell everybody you're thirty-nine but you're really forty."

Mom's eyes widened in surprise.

I tried to change the subject. "People magazine wrote that every girl in the world would love to have the last, slow song at a dance with Justin Adams."

"That's nice," the flight attendant said. It was obvious she still didn't know who Justin was. "Most people go to Disney World to see Mickey Mouse."

Laura kept giving Susan a how-long-have-you-been-away-from-Earth? look. I picked up my bag and nudged her in the ribs, hoping she'd get the message and stop.

"Ow," Laura complained.

"There's our boarding call," Susan said. "We have to get going."

Mom gave me a huge hug. "I'm going to miss you, darling."

"Sorry about what Laura said," I whispered to her.

"It's all right," she whispered back. "I'm surprised you noticed. And I'm surprised you talk about things like that with your friends."

"Just with my best friend," I told her. "Only with Laura."

Mom released me and smiled at Laura.

"In spite of your comments about my age, I'm going to miss you too, Laura. You have certainly changed the atmosphere of our apartment these last few weeks. Our home is such a lively place when you visit. It's going to be very quiet without you around."

Laura tugged at her curls. "Britt says there's a good thing about us going away, Mrs. P. She says you and your boyfriend, Kevin, will be able to do whatever you want without her hanging around."

Mom glared at me as if Laura's big mouth was my fault.

"I like you hanging around when Kevin visits," Mom said to me. "It's not like he's a serious boyfriend or anything."

"That's not what Britt thinks," Laura announced. "She says you've been going out with him for eight months. She says you always give Kevin a long kiss when he leaves. She says you and him are really serious."

Mom's eyes squinted into tight lines. "You're certainly noticing a lot more now that you're growing up, Brittany."

"This is our boarding call," Susan interrupted us.

Mom kissed my forehead. "Enjoy yourself. And do what your father says. You know how he can worry about things. Don't give him anything to worry about."

"I won't," I promised.

Mom kissed me again. Then she gave Laura a quick hug and kiss. "Watch out for each other."

* * * * *

"How could you say those things in front of Mom and the stewardess?" I asked as our plane taxied slowly from the terminal.

Laura pulled her seatbelt tighter. "That's the second time you've asked me and I still don't understand why it bothered you. Your mom lying about her age is sort of funny, when you think about it. I mean, what's the difference between thirty-nine and forty? They're both old."

"It's not really old," I pointed out. "You know adults don't like to be reminded how old they are. For some reason it bothers them. I could tell my mother was embarrassed. And she was embarrassed about Kevin too."

"Why?" Laura said. "She likes him, right? Besides, if it's such a big secret, why would you tell me?"

"Because we're friends. What I tell you is between friends. It doesn't mean I want you blabbing it all over. Do you understand?"

"No."

"Laura, I . . . "

"But I understand it upsets you," she interrupted. "Just like when I told Lucy-Mae Bennett you thought she was a slimy witch."

"I got mad at you because I didn't say anything like that."

"Okay, you said you hated her slimy guts. Same thing."

"That's not true either. My exact words were, 'She's stuck up.' Your translation got me in deep doo-doo with Lucy-Mae. She'll probably never speak to me again."

"Then you should be thanking me," Laura reasoned. "Look, I know me yapping to Lucy-Mae bugged you."

"Because it was embarrassing," I insisted.

"I'll try harder to think before I say something that might embarrass you," Laura promised. "Okay?"

"A deal, " I agreed.

She held out her right hand and we shook on it. Suddenly she gripped my hand tighter. "Why has the plane stopped, Britt? Is there something wrong with the engines?"

I shook my head and peeled her fingers

off my palm. "We're just waiting for our turn on the runway. So many planes use this airport, there's usually a wait to take off."

"Oh." She fidgeted in her seat.

"Are you all right? You seem nervous."

"I am," she confessed. "A little. Well, maybe more than a little. This is the first time I've flown anywhere. My family always drives. This plane is super big. I don't see how it can get off the ground."

"I felt the same way the first time I went to visit my dad, three years ago. I spent the whole flight pulling on the armrests. I thought that would help hold the plane up. Stupid, huh?"

"Yeah, stupid," Laura agreed with a fake laugh. Her knuckles went white as she pulled on her armrests.

"My dad says that planes are the safest way to travel." I tried to reassure her. "He says you're fourteen times as likely to have an accident driving to the airport as you are on the plane."

"I'd rather sit in the front," Laura said. "I hear it's safer in the front of a plane if there's a crash. We're in the second-last row."

That didn't make any sense to me. "I don't think there's any safe seats in a crash.

Whenever they show a plane disaster on the news, everything is completely mangled up."

"Thanks. I needed to know that. Now I feel a whole lot better. Aren't you nervous, Britt?"

"I was the first time. But I've been to Florida three times now. I find flying sort of boring."

"I don't mean flying. Are you nervous about seeing your father?"

"Talking to you is like riding a roller coaster," I said. "You change directions so fast."

"When did you see him last?"

"A year ago Christmas."

"That's a long time," Laura said. "If you were a fruit fly, you'd have been dead over . . . let's see . . . you would have been dead over two thousand years. Fruit fly years that is."

"Fruit fly years? What are you talking about?"

"Remember what Mr. Fitzgerald said in Science last week? He said fruit flies only live for two weeks."

"What has that got to do with anything?

"Simple. A fruit fly lives fourteen days. That means one day in the life of a fruit fly is like five years to us. So a year and three months . . . .that's when you saw your dad last . . . is about . . . er . . . almost five hundred days, right? Five hundred days times five fruit-fly-years a day is twenty-five hundred years. If you were a fruit fly, you'd have been dead for twenty-five centuries. Just think of that. You'd sort of be a King Tut to fruit flies."

"If I was a fruit fly? Only you could think of something so . . . so . . . stupid."

"Thanks," she said and we both laughed.

It was good minute before we could stop laughing. "We'd better settle down," I suggested. "If we laugh like this in Florida, it'll drive my father crazy. Remember, I told you how uptight he is."

"About your dad," Laura said. "It must be weird not seeing him for so long."

"It is. I was eleven then. I had short hair."

"I know. You showed me your sixth grade class photo. Your hair looks much better long. I bet your dad is going to notice more changes than just your hair, though."

"Like what?"

"Like how much you've grown. Plus you were really flat in the class photo."

"I was what?"

"You've grown a lot that way too."

"Do you have to tell the whole world?" I whispered through my teeth.

"Well, you have," she went on. "It's tough on fathers when their daughters fill out. When it happened to me, my dad seemed afraid to hug me. Like he thought I was all grown up and I didn't want to be hugged anymore."

"You're speaking too loud. I don't think other people want to hear this." I was still whispering through my teeth.

"I'm talking loud?"

I nodded.

She looked at the other passengers. "Sorry. Nobody's listening. Old people can't hear all that well," she said in a softer voice. "And I bet he'll treat you differently."

The plane moved onto the runway and the jet engines whined as the plane picked up speed. The whine quickly turned into a roar and the 767 began to bounce as it tore down the runway.

"Oh, no," Laura moaned. "We're going to die."

Chapter Three

Toilets and Trees

Laura clamped her hands on the armrests and tensed her muscles. "Why is it going so fast?" she squeaked.

"It goes this fast to take off," I told her.

"It does? It's not going fast because it's crashing?" Her voice turned from soprano into falsetto.

"Think about it, Laura. How can we crash when we're still on the ground? This is normal."

"This is normal?"

"Everything is fine."

"Everything is fine?"

"Did someone offer you a job as a parrot?" I teased.

A loud thud vibrated through our sneakers.

"Didthebottomjustfallofftheplane?"

Laura said the sentence as if it was one word.

I forced myself to stifle a laugh.

"That's just the wheels pulling up. We're in the air." I glanced out the window. "We're as high as the clouds already. Take a look."

"No, thanks," she said as she flipped the buckle on her seat belt and stood up.

"Where are you going?" I asked.

"To the bathroom. When I'm nervous, I have to go bad."

I pointed at the panel above our heads. "You're not supposed to get up until the seat belt sign goes off."

Susan, the fight attendant, fumbled down the aisle from the front of the plane. She grabbed the back of the seats for balance. "You have to sit down," she ordered. Then she repeated what I'd said about the seat belt sign.

Laura shook her head. "When I'm nervous I have to go to the toilet. Seat belt sign or no seat belt sign, I just have to go."

"Can't you wait?" Susan asked.

"I have to go humongus bad," Laura insisted.

Susan sighed a frustrated, "All right," and helped Laura toward the washroom at the back of the plane. I heard the lock on the toilet door slide shut.

Susan sat beside me to wait. She drummed her fingers on the armrest. "It's lucky you and your friend are sitting so close to the toilet. People don't realize how steep a climb we're in during takeoff. We once had a gentleman stand up during a takeoff and he rolled down the aisle. He simply rolled down. Fortunately, he wasn't hurt."

The image made me want to smile. I didn't. The look on Susan's face told me she didn't find it amusing.

"Must have shocked him," I said.

"You can say that again. People should understand that the rules we have are for their own safety. They think . . . "

"Aaarrrggghhh!" The bathroom door crashed open and Laura charged out.

I jumped in surprise. So did all the other passengers around me.

The button and zipper on Laura's jeans were open and her T-shirt was half tucked in.

Susan stood up. "What's wrong?"

"The toilet!" Laura shouted. "I almost got sucked down the toilet. I was sitting there and pulled the little handle thing and swooossshhh, there was this gigantic, sucking noise. If I hadn't stood up real fast, I would have been sucked down there."

The other passengers shifted in their seats and tried not to smile. "That noise is perfectly normal," Susan explained. "That's the way a toilet flushes on a Boeing 767."

"You're kidding!" Laura said in disbelief. "That big fluuussshhh is the way it's supposed to be?"

"Absolutely," Susan said. "Now I must insist you sit down."

"Nobody ever gets sucked down the toilet?" Laura asked as she eased into her seat.

"Of course not." Susan shook her head. "Please remain seated until the seat belt sign goes off."

We watched Susan stumble her way back to the front of the plane.

"Your jeans are undone," I said.

Laura fixed her clothing.

"Are you embarrassed?" I asked. "Everybody was looking at you."

"Of course I'm not embarrassed. I'm angry," she snarled. "I thought I was being sucked down a toilet. Have you ever been sucked down a toilet before?"

"Not that I can remember. But somebody probably was . . . in an R. L. Stine novel."

And we were laughing again.

* * * * *

Laura and I had to wait until the other passengers got off before Susan allowed us to leave the plane. We followed her through the Miami airport to the baggage pick-up. Laura seemed happy to have landed safely. Or happy to be in Florida. Or happy to be closer to Justin Adams. Whatever, she strolled along showing lots of braces.

There was a big crowd in the waiting area, but I spotted Dad right away. He stood on the other side of the rail with his forehead squashed into worry-wrinkles.

I waved to him and the wrinkles smoothed a little.

Dad hadn't changed much in fifteen months. He looked a little thinner on top and maybe he'd put on some weight, but he was, in my opinion, still incredibly handsome for someone over forty.

Dad says that first impressions are extremely important in the accident investigation business, so he spends a lot of time on his appearance. His hair, what's left of it, is always neatly cut. He shaves twice a day, so there's never any whisker stubble.

And he has his suits made to measure.

Susan helped us gather our suitcases. She showed the security guard our baggage claim checks and escorted us to my father.

"I was so worried," was the first thing Dad said. "I thought you'd missed the plane. Those were special discount tickets. They were only good for that one flight. I was . . ."

"Dad." I stopped him. "We're here."

Dad thanked Susan for helping us. She said a polite "Good-bye," and disappeared into the crowd.

Dad looked me up and down and seemed unsure of what he should do next. So I reached out and hugged him. "I've really missed you," I said.

"And I've missed you too," he said. "You look . . . different."

"Told you he'd notice," Laura whispered.

"I'm different? What do you mean, Dad?"

"Well, I . . . er . . . I didn't know you'd had your ears pierced. Aren't you too young to have pierced ears?"

"Mom doesn't think so. She gave them to me for my twelfth birthday," I said.

"I had my ears pierced in kindergarten," Laura announced. "Half the boys in our seventh grade homeroom have their ears pierced. It's no big deal, Mr. Prentice."

Dad regarded Laura with a confused expression. I figured it was time to introduce her.

Dad and Laura shook hands. "Pleased to meet you," they said at the same time.

"I really appreciate you inviting me along, sir," Laura said. "I've never been to Florida before."

"It's my pleasure," Dad told her. "I've been promising to take Brittany to Walt Disney World for the last three years. I thought she'd enjoy it even more if she had a friend along."

"Yeah, Britt and I are really looking forward to it, Mr. P. You think we'll be able to see Justin Adams?"

"Justin Adams?" Dad looked puzzled. "Isn't he that child actor on that silly show in the burger restaurant?"

"It's not a silly show, sir. It's the most-watched TV show in the world. It's translated into thirty-seven languages. And Justin's not a child," Laura said. "He was thirteen last week. That makes him a teenager."

"Oh, that one," Dad said. "I was thinking of the cute little boy. The one with the freckles."

"Justin Adams is cuter than Little Mike Pierce," Laura declared. "Their show is taped at . . . "

I stopped her. "We can tell Dad about that later. Let's get out of the airport."

Dad brushed his hand across my hair the way you'd do to a toddler. "You sure have grown up. You've . . . you've . . . "

"Filled out," Laura volunteered.

"Yes," he agreed. "Quite the change." Then he mussed my hair again. "But you'll always be my little girl, even if you have pierced ears."

"Don't do that," I complained. "Don't mess up my hair."

My father reached over and gently pressed his hand to the middle of my back. "Stand up straight, Brittany. You're slouching. You know how important it is to have good posture. It allows your internal organs to breathe."

I pulled away from him. "This is more than embarrassing, Dad."

"Well, I'll be embarrassed if I have a daughter who slouches." He leaned closer to study my face.

"What?" I said defensively. "What are you looking at?"

"The paint on your face," he answered.

"Paint?" I frowned.

"You're wearing make-up, aren't you?"

I nodded. "Just a little gloss and shadow."

"Does your mother know?" he challenged.

"Of course. I've been wearing make-up since last fall. It's not much."

"Britt has such deep brown eyes." Laura said. "The eye shadow makes her look even more . . . mysterious."

"Twelve-year-olds are not supposed to look mysterious," Dad said. "I don't like it, Brittany. Earrings? Make-up? You're too young for such things."

"Dad . . . "

"Your mother," my father mumbled under his breath. Then he said, "We'll discuss it later." He picked up our suitcases. "I'm parked out here. I suppose we should get some lunch. Are you hungry?"

"You bet," Laura said. "They tried to serve us this yucky Eggs Benedict stuff on the plane."

"A lot of people consider Eggs Benedict a classy breakfast," Dad pointed out.

"Then a lot of people have no taste," Laura affirmed. "It was disgusting. Let's hit the Baron Burger Court."

"Baron Burger Court?" Dad looked confused.

"That's the name of the restaurant on Justin Adams's TV show, sir," Laura explained. "Wouldn't you just die if you walked into a restaurant, ordered a cheeseburger, then had Justin Adams walk up and ask, 'Do you want fries with that?'? I mean, wouldn't you just die?"

"I don't think so, Laura," Dad answered dryly.

"Are we going back to your apartment?" I asked.

My father shook his head. "No time. We're going to take our little trip through the Everglades. That will take a couple of hours. Then we'll drive to Orlando. That'll take us a while. It'll be late by the time we get there. But tomorrow morning, we'll be fresh for Disney World."

"Sounds great," Laura said. "Are we going to stay at a hotel with a swimming pool?"

"There will be a pool," Dad told us. "But it'll be better than a hotel. I have a friend who has a condo in Orlando. She gave me the key and told me we're welcome to use her place for the whole five days we're there."

"She?" I asked.

"Just a friend," Dad said.

The automatic door slid open and we walked toward the parking lot.

"Hey, this is terrific, Mr. P," Laura exclaimed. "It's warm. It's like summer. To think that there's still snow on the ground in Toronto and it feels like July here. Wow, look at that." She pointed to the far side of the parking lot.

I couldn't see anything, just lots of cars, a fence and a border of trees.

"What are we supposed to be looking at?"

"The trees," Laura gasped.

"The trees?" Dad and I chorused.

"Yeah, the trees," she said. "They're palm trees. I've never, ever seen a palm tree before. Well, I have in pictures and on TV and stuff. But I've never seen a real palm tree before."

"Well, you should get used to them. Laura. There's all kinds of palm trees down here," Dad said.

"I have to go touch one," Laura said. "I'll just be a minute."

She jogged over to the row of trees.

"What is she doing?" Dad asked in surprise.

Laura ran up to the biggest tree. Instead of just touching it, she threw her arms around it and rubbed her face gently against the bark.

An elderly couple walking to their car stopped to gaze at my strange friend.

"What is she doing?" Dad repeated.

"You might as well know this right away, Dad. Laura is a little different from normal people."

"You can say that again." I'm sure he was wondering if he had made a mistake sending the extra ticket.

Chapter Four

A Squashed Skunk?

Laura described her close encounter with the tree as we exited the parking lot. "It wasn't rough at all. It was kind of smooth. Nothing like an oak or a maple."

I sat in the front with Dad while Laura leaned forward and poked her head between us from the back seat.

"That was a royal palm," Dad said. "Most of the other types aren't smooth. Do you often hug trees, Laura?"

She chuckled. "I guess I must have looked pretty dumb, huh?"

"Let's say you looked a little unusual," Dad answered diplomatically. "I don't think I know anybody else who hugs trees."

"I'm a bit of a goof sometimes," Laura confessed. "Aren't I, Britt?"

"Yes," I agreed. "Sometimes more than a bit."

"But I always figure it's better to be a bit too goofy than a bit too serious. What do you think, Mr. Prentice?"

"I think that's an interesting point of view, Laura," my father observed. "Is your seat belt on?"

Dad made a few turns and soon we were driving along Highway 41, the Tamiami Trail, which connects Miami on the Atlantic side to Naples on the Gulf of Mexico and goes through the Everglades.

"How is Noda?" Dad asked.

"Fine," I answered. "The same old, stupid cat."

"Cats aren't stupid," Laura interjected. "Cats are really smart. Suppose it's minus ten degrees and a blizzard is blowing off Lake Ontario. You say, 'Okay, Bootsie, it's time to go outside.' What does the cat do?"

"Go outside?" I guessed.

"Of course not. It goes insane. It turns into a screaming mass of fur and claws and teeth and runs under the bed and stays there. That's smart."

"I guess so." Dad sounded slightly bewildered.

We sat in silence for a few minutes.

Then Laura leaned forward and poked me. "Hey, Brittany, look at that!"

"What?"

"That bus driver — he was picking his nose." She snorted. "Does he think he's invisible in there?"

My father cleared his throat. Laura leaned closer. "Hey, Mr. Prentice, do you know you can make fake boogers from rubber cement?"

"Pardon?"

"Yeah, you spread a little rubber cement on your desk, let it dry, then start to roll it. It peels off in these little pieces that look like real boogers."

"Pardon me?" Dad stiffened up.

Just like on the plane, I had to stifle a laugh. "How did you figure that out?" I couldn't help asking.

"In fifth grade, one of the boys grossed out a sub by sticking rubber cement boogers all over his math sheet. Disgusting, huh? But funny at the same time . . . when you think about it."

I couldn't hold it in any longer and began chuckling.

Dad scolded me with his eyes. "It's just disgusting," he affirmed.

"But it's funny," Laura repeated.

I watched Dad's worry lines fold into deep creases. Now I was *sure* he thought he'd made a mistake sending me two tickets.

Soon Dad pulled off the highway in front of a sign which read: A-1 EVERGLADES AIR-BOAT RIDES. "Are you girls up for a fast ride through the Everglades?" he asked. "Maybe we'll get to see an alligator or two."

"All right," Laura exclaimed. "An alligator. I've never seen a real alligator before."

"Well, you're going to have to make me a promise," Dad warned her. "If we do see one, you're going to have to promise you won't try to hug it."

Laura let go a belly laugh. "Hey, that was a good one, Mr. Prentice. That was really funny. I didn't think you'd be this funny. Britt told me you were uptight most of the time. She said you had the same sense of humor as a doorknob."

I just buried my head in my hands, groaned and waited for my father to park the car.

*****

"I have to go inside the souvenir shop to buy the tickets for the boat ride," Dad said. "Why don't you come and look at the tourist souvenirs while I do that? Most of it is, to be polite, junk, but you might find something interesting."

Laura and I turned to each other and shook our heads in unison. "Naw," we said together.

"It'll be more fun down there," I told Dad. "We'll go wait by the dock."

Dad squinted and checked out the canal which cut through the trees and shrubs to the left of the parking lot. There was a wooden dock jutting into the water. A girl about kindergarten age and her parents were watching fish jump among the lilies.

"Yeah, let's go throw stones at the fish," Laura suggested. Then she saw the expression on my father's face. "That's a joke, Mr. P. I wouldn't throw anything at a fish. Honest. I like fish. I like fish a whole lot. If I'm ever reincarnated, that means born again in another life, I want to come back as a fish. It would be sort of neat to have scales and breathe in water and . . . " she pointed at her temples, "have eyes that are here."

"I suppose so," Dad mumbled. He pointed at the door of the souvenir shop. "Still, I'd rather you came with me. I don't want you going to the dock alone."

"Why?" I asked.

"It's just that I'd feel better being there

"It's just that I'd feel better being there with you."

"Why?" I asked again.

"That should be obvious, Brittany. A dock is a dangerous place. You could hurt yourself."

"How?"

He sighed in frustration. "You could fall into the water."

"I'm not going to fall in the water," I told him. "And even if I do, I know how to swim. I've got my blue badge from the Y. Besides, it doesn't look deep. There's all kinds of lilies on the surface."

"We'll be okay, Mr. Prentice," Laura said. "We won't goof around or nothing. We'll just watch the fish and maybe throw the little kid in." She paused a moment. "That's a joke too."

"I don't want to worry about you two while I'm buying the tickets," he said. "You can come with me into the souvenir shop or wait here by the car."

"Dad, do you remember what I wrote in my letter? I've taken the CPR course. That's short for Cardiopulmonary Resuscitation."

"Britt knows how to help somebody breathe if they're not breathing and keep their heart beating even if their heart has stopped," Laura completed the explanation.

"I know what it means," he snapped. "And I don't think children need to know those sorts of things."

"Margo, my instructor, said I'm the perfect age to learn CPR," I said. "She says if everybody knew it, we could save a lot of people who have had heart attacks. Mom says she's proud of me."

"Your mother," he mumbled again. "Why do we want to make our kids grow up so fast nowadays?"

There was a hint of sweat on my father's scalp. That meant he was starting to get angry. When he gets mad he makes his demon face.

My father's demon face is a pretty terrifying sight. His scalp gets covered with beady sweat beneath his thinning hair. His eyes show all kinds of white and little throbbing veins appear on his temples. I've always thought Dad would have made a perfect junior high school assistant principal. Nobody would ever be a discipline problem if they knew they'd be sent to the office to confront the demon face.

Dad wasn't impressed by my swimming or first-aid knowledge. "It doesn't help to know CPR if you're the person who's drowned."

"But Dad . . . "

"But Dad nothing," he snapped. "I am your father and I'm responsible for your safety. I don't want to spend the entire week arguing with you. Do you understand me, Brittany?"

"I just . . . "

"Do you understand, Brittany?" His lips were moving, but he kept his teeth together.

"Yes, Dad."

"Good." With that, he turned and marched into the store.

As soon as the door closed behind him, Laura said, "You were right. He *is* sort of uptight."

"Enough," I snarled.

"I agree. Your dad is being pretty picky. He's treating us like little kids."

"Yeah, but it's you I've had enough of. Can't you keep your mouth shut?"

"Me?" Laura looked shocked. "What did I say wrong?"

"In the car. You told my dad I said he was uptight most of the time."

She nodded her head in the direction of the shop door. "I've only known him for less than an hour, but he sure seems that way."

"But it's like with my mom at the airport. You don't tell him that. How do you think it makes me feel? I wanted *you* to know it, not my dad."

She sucked her breath through her teeth and punched her forehead. "I'm sorry, Britt. I did it again, didn't I? I'm a jerk. Forgive me. I'm not thinking right today. I guess the excitement of being so close to Justin Adams is making me a bit loony."

"You can say that again."

"Don't be mad at me, huh? Look, I'll keep my mouth shut from now on." She thought for a second. "No, I can't do that. I'd go nuts. But I *will* think before I say anything. And if it looks like I'm going to blab something dumb, then pull on your earring. I'll get the clue and zip up right away. Okay?"

I bit my bottom lip and stared at her.

"Friends?" she pleaded. "Please?"

I continued to give her the evil eye.

Laura grinned and the Florida sun sparkled off her braces. "Please. Pretty please. Pretty please with a squashed skunk on top."

"A squashed skunk?"

"You smiled." She slapped my arm. "I saw you. Your lips twitched. You smiled."

"Did not," I growled.

"Yes, you did. Come on, Britt. Give me another chance. I won't mess you up again. And if you see me heading for trouble, you've got the signal. Please."

"All right," I grumbled. "One more chance."

But, to tell the truth, it wasn't really Laura's comment in the car that had upset me.

It was Dad.

As Laura said, he was treating me like a little kid. And I didn't like that at all.

Chapter Five

Affagators

Laura and I waited for Dad in silence. She spent the time grabbing at love bugs, small black flies that fly stupidly into your face. I leaned against the car, stewing about my father's attitude. A couple of times I was spooked by large, black wasps buzzing by.

"We're in luck," Dad said when he returned. "Apparently, the boat is due back at any moment. Let's go wait on the dock."

His prediction was correct. Almost immediately, the sound of a racing engine thundered down the canal. The little girl covered her ears as an airboat appeared and glided up to the dock.

"What a weird-looking boat," Laura yelled in my ear.

It was flat like a raft. At the rear, about

a meter in the air, was an automobile engine. Attached to the back of it was an enormous fan, as big as an airplane propeller, which blew the boat forward. The driver sat directly in front of it, also way up in the air. Three benches full of tourists stretched across the front of the raft.

The engine coughed to a stop and the passengers filed off.

"Quite the ride," an elderly gentleman said to me.

"Hop on, folks," the driver called to us. "My name is Allan. I'm your skilled and trained airboat pilot. You're in safe hands. I have over sixty seconds of experience driving this thing."

Dad chuckled at the corny joke. Laura and I gave each other scrunched-face looks.

Dad stood to one side to let the little girl and her parents take the front bench. That's where I wanted to sit, but I knew it was polite to let the little kid have the best seat.

Even though I could do it myself, Dad held my arm while I climbed on. Then he followed me and held Laura's hand as she jumped aboard. "You girls can sit on the sides," he said.

"Port side is the best," Allan the driver told us. "That's the left side to you landlubbers. That's where you'll get closest to the alligators."

"Great," I said. "Guess I'm sitting in first class."

"Trade places with me," Dad instructed. "Let me sit there."

"No way. I got this seat. You get stuck in the middle."

I thought Dad was joking with me. But he wasn't. "Trade now," he ordered. He stood up and shifted in front of me. I was forced into the middle.

"Why did you do that?" I complained.

"I think it's better that I sit here if we're going to get close to alligators. You can never tell what might happen. It's the safest thing. I don't want anything to happen to my little girl, do I?"

I blushed with embarrassment. What did the other family think? It made me feel even worse when the father in the front bench traded with his daughter. He moved so she was sitting on the left.

"Sit up straight, Brittany," Dad ordered. "You're slouching again."

"Welcome aboard A-1 Everglades Airboat Rides," the driver announced. "You are a passenger on a boat which can float on only four inches of water. That's good to know, because a foot is considered deep water around here. Power is supplied by the Cadillac engine behind me. The fan pushes us forward. We can't use a regular propeller because it would get choked with grass and weeds, as you will shortly see. Now, if you just hold up your tickets so I know you're not stowaways, we'll be on our way."

The engine screamed into life. The boat pitched sharply into the canal and we roared into the Everglades.

"Whew," Laura shouted. "All right. All right!"

I was going to protest to Dad some more, but the ride was so thrilling I temporarily forgot my humiliation. The wind ripped into my face and made my eyes water. The bushes on the side of the canal rushed past in a green blur.

"Hey, Britt," Laura yelled. "Look at this."

She opened her mouth so the wind made her cheeks flap. The sides of her face vibrated, making a popping noise loud enough to be heard above the overpowering drone of the engine.

"It's fun," Laura shouted. "It makes your head tingle. Try it."

I smiled at her. It looked funny. And no

doubt it was fun. But there was no way I was going to do it. I remembered the wasps back at the car. The last thing I needed was a mouthful of them.

There was a break in the bushes and Allan steered the airboat out of the canal into what looked like a huge, flat field of grass. We quickly discovered that the grass was growing in a shallow sea of water. The airboat increased speed and raced forward. Allan steered a little left, then a little right, left, right, so that the airboat swayed in dizzy waves.

"This is great," Laura exclaimed. "This is making me feel sick. I feel like I'm going to chuck. This is great."

The wind on my face forced tears from my eyes. The world became a fuzzy green carpet. The air was warm and musty, and the watery smell of the Everglades pushed up my nose. It was a terrific feeling. The first two weeks of March had been so cold in Toronto. It had even snowed. At that moment, I was sure glad to be where I was.

Suddenly, the scream of the engine dropped to a put-putter and the nose of the airboat dipped into the water-grass, throwing us gently forward. Laura and the little kid squealed with delight.

"I slowed down because we're coming to the alligators and I don't want to spook them," Allan said from the driver's seat above our heads. "Anybody got any questions so far?"

"Why doesn't it look like a swamp?" Laura asked. "I thought it was going to be more boggy. Lots of moss hanging from spooky-looking trees. And big dragonflies and ugly bugs and The Swamp Thing like in the comic book. Stuff like that."

"It is in spots," Allan explained. "A little more to the north. And it's not really a swamp. It's a fifty-mile-wide river which runs from Lake Okeechobee into the Gulf of Mexico. Part of it forms Everglades National Park, the third largest national park in America."

"Does it ever flood?" I wondered.

"Believe it or not, we worry about too little rather than too much water," Allan went on. "We've had a lot of rain this year. When we have a drought, these wetlands vanish. Sometimes the peat bogs are so dry they catch on fire."

"That's weird, huh?" Laura said. "I can't picture a swamp burning up."

The engine stopped. "Let's be quiet now, folks," Allan instructed. "You see the clump of bushes on the left? There's a little pothole beside it. You should be able to see . . . "

"There!" the little kid shouted. "See it, Mommy. There's an affagator."

"Look at that thing," Dad whispered.

"Wowzer," I muttered under my breath. "What a huge animal."

The alligator was at least two meters long, probably more. It floated on the surface of the water, unmoving. As the boat drifted closer, the reptile raised its head and opened its massive jaws with a soft hiss.

I leaned forward to get a closer look. Dad held out his arm to stop me. "Don't get too close, Brittany," he warned.

"That's right," Allan added. "These things have been known to jump six feet into the air and land right in the middle of the boat."

Dad stiffened so quickly that his outstretched arm knocked me back into the seat.

"That hurt," I protested.

"Just kidding, folks," Allan continued. "There is absolutely no danger. Just don't dangle your hand in the water or you might go home missing a few fingers."

"That hurt," I repeated.

"Sorry," Dad said. "I thought you might fall in."

The boat drifted slowly in a half circle so the right side drew close to the alligator.

"And I was just kidding about the best seats," Allan said. "I think the folks on the right should get as good a view."

I noticed Dad wasn't making any effort to protect Laura from getting too close.

Laura pointed at a log behind the alligator. "There's little ones. There's babies."

"That's right," Allan told us. "Alligators protect their young. They're good parents."

"I bet they don't overprotect them," I grumped under my breath.

Chapter Six

Emerald Place

"You haven't said much since the airboat ride, Brittany," Dad said as we passed the Orlando city limits sign. "Almost four hours with only the occasional grunt isn't like you. Cat got your tongue?"

I've always thought that was a dumb expression. "Yes," I told him. "The dumb cat has got my dumb tongue."

"Ouch," Laura said.

"There's absolutely no need to be rude," Dad lectured.

After Allan had returned us to the dock, I walked directly to the car and claimed the back seat. I gave my father the silent treatment during the long ride to Orlando.

Laura, on the other hand, had spent the drive bewildering my father with her observations of the people in our homeroom class.

"Clancy picks his nose with his pen . . .

"Amy sticks paper towels in her sweat shirt . . .

"Lucy-Mae thinks she's so beautiful, but she really looks like a frog . . .

"Pedro sounds like a wounded horse when he laughs . . .

"Leroy's eyebrows grow together so he looks like a werewolf . . ."

I would have liked to add my comments, but there was no way I was going to be even halfway sociable to my dad.

Dad turned the car off the highway, drove a short way down a residential street and through the wrought iron gates of a condominium complex. A large wooden sign told us we were in Emerald Place.

"We're here," he announced.

"This is awesome," Laura said. "It reminds me of *The Wizard of Oz*."

We parked in front of a strange-looking townhouse. It was like something you'd see in a science fiction movie, something from in the future. Like most of the other places we'd passed in the neighborhood, the condo was made of stucco, but the windows were placed at odd angles. They seemed too big or too small, or sideways when they should have been lengthwise. At first, it did look like it belonged in Munchkin Land. But the more I looked at it, the more it grew on me.

"This place has won all kinds of architectural design awards," Dad told us.

"Looks like it was built by aliens," Laura said.

"An unusual thought," Dad mused. "Whatever, it's ours for the week, and it's only ten miles from Disney World. There's also a pool and a hot tub."

"Decent," Laura exclaimed.

"This is our unit right in front of us," Dad went on. "I want to shower and shave. Why don't you girls watch TV while you're waiting? When I'm finished, we'll go to Perkins for supper."

"Let's go for a swim instead," Laura suggested. "Would that be okay, Mr. Prentice?"

Dad shook his head. "No, I don't think so. There isn't a lifeguard."

"We both know how to swim," I pointed out. "Remember, I have my blue badge?" This sounded like a replay of the boat dock.

Laura supported me. "That's right. We'll watch each other."

"Accidents happen this fast." Dad snapped his fingers.

"We'll stay in the shallow end," Laura pleaded. "Honest, Mr. P, we'll be fine."

"You'll stay in the shallow end?" he asked.

"If you want us to," I grumbled.

"Sure," Laura said.

"All right," Dad said reluctantly. "But I'm going to leave the bathroom window open a little. If anything goes wrong, I'll be able to hear you."

* * * * *

We were the only people in the pool. An old lady with skin so wrinkled she could have played a part in a California Raisin commercial walked by and made an ugly face.

"Maybe she thinks we're going to pee in the pool," Laura said after she left.

We splashed around in the shallow end for a few minutes, but the water was surprisingly cold.

"I thought everything in Florida was supposed to be hot," Laura complained.

We bundled ourselves in beach towels and scrunched into a couple of deck chairs. The sun set quickly and soon the air seemed as cool as the water.

Laura pointed at the frosted bathroom window of our borrowed condo. It was open a few centimeters. "Your Dad must have stayed here before. How would he know the bathroom was on the same side as the pool?"

I was still in a snarky mood. "My father knows everything."

"Do you want to go inside?" Laura asked. "Maybe there's a rerun of *Do You Want Fries With That?* on one of the local channels. Watching Justin Adams will warm us up."

"No, thanks. I'm going to stay here for a few minutes," I told her. "I'm finding it sort of difficult to spend time with my father right now."

She nodded sympathetically. "I can tell. He's being a little overwhelming. Me saying that is okay, isn't it? You're not tugging your earring."

"This time you're right," I said.

"Making you sit in the middle on the boat was so weird. And the fuss he made over your earrings and make-up was so old-fashioned. He'd be really surprised if he saw the rest of the girls in our class, huh? If he saw Lucy-Mae Bennett, he'd flip out. My folks would never let me wear the make-up and clothes Lucy-Mae wears. Don't you think she looks sixteen?"

"You know how I feel about Lucy-Mae," I said. "What am I going to do about my dad, Laura?"

She thought for a moment. "Why don't

you tell him how you feel?" she suggested. "Talk to him daughter to father. Tell him to let you have a little slack."

"He'll only get mad at me like in the souvenir shop."

"But you weren't talking then," she pointed out. "You were arguing."

I scowled and then looked away. I watched the underwater lights shimmer in the gentle waves of the pool. "You're right. I was. But I had a good reason. My father is such a worrier."

"Talk to him," she repeated. "It's better than arguing. And it's a lot better than pouting, like you were in the car. I believe in talking."

"I wasn't pouting. I was sulking. There's a difference. Little kids pout."

"Whatever you call it, Britt, it was pretty silly. The way I figure it, giving your dad the silent treatment sure won't impress him with your maturity."

I glared angrily at her and then realized she was right. I wanted Dad to stop treating me like a little kid and all afternoon I'd acted like one. Pretty dumb. "All right. I was being silly. But so was my father. He's always been uptight. There used to be a 7-Eleven on the corner near our old house.

It was a one-minute bike ride. Dad wouldn't let me go alone."

"How old were you then?"

"Third grade."

"That doesn't seem all that unreasonable to me, Britt. I've only been in Toronto a couple of months and I've seen lots of weird-looking people walking around."

"I could never, ever go to the mall," I went on complaining. "Even if a whole bunch of kids was going, I couldn't go. Dad would *worry* about me."

"That doesn't sound unreasonable either. You were a little kid then. Look, stop upsetting yourself; think about something else. You're in Disney World for a week. It's warm . . . " she pulled the beach towel tighter around her. " . . . well, it's warm in the daytime anyway. You're on vacation. Tomorrow you're going to see the terminally cute Justin Adams. Sure, your father is acting strict, but he hasn't seen you in fifteen months. Give him a few days to see you've changed, that you've grown up a whole lot. And while you're waiting, have a little fun."

"Just like a teacher," I mumbled under my breath.

"What?"

"You just gave me a lecture."

"I did? Sorry."

I nodded. "I'm freezing under this towel. I have goosebumps on my goosebumps. Let's go inside to warm up."

"Agreed," she said. "Say, do you think I'm being stupid about Justin Adams? I mean, I really think we're going to see him. If I don't, I'll die. I'll simply fade away. A day without Justin Adams is like a day without corn flakes."

"Like a day without orange juice," I added.

"Right. Like a day without ice cream."

"Like a day without sunshine," I went on.

She grinned. "Like a day without a BM."

"A what?"

"A BM. You know, short for a bowel movement. It's all my grandma talks about."

"That's disgusting, Laura."

"But true," she said.

And, once more, we started laughing.

Chapter Seven

A Little Child?

When Lucy-Mae Bennett came back from Disney World last year, she told the class it was "really, really big." But I didn't understand how big was really, really big until I saw it. It's huge. Gigantic. It's like a city.

It has its own four-lane highway system, its own bus service. There's a monorail train which travels about seven meters off the ground and connects the theme parks. The parking lot is so humongus, you'd almost believe all the cars in North America would fit in. And that's how many cars seemed to be parked there when we arrived after breakfast.

"We're parking an awful long way from the gates," Laura noted as Dad followed the directions of what seemed like a hundred parking attendants. "Can't we get any closer, Mr. P? We have to walk so far we're going to be too tired to see Justin Adams."

Dad smiled for the first time since we'd arrived in Florida. "We don't have to walk. They have a tram that drives around to pick us up."

The tram delivered us to the gates in a couple of minutes. We stood in line at the ticket booth for a few more minutes, bought passes for five days, and then entered.

"Which way is the studio?" Laura wanted to know.

Dad pointed back toward the highway. "That way. Today, we'll catch the monorail and go across the river to the Magic Kingdom."

"Magic Kingdom?" Laura sounded disappointed. "We're not going to the movie studios?"

"We'll visit Mickey Mouse and Donald Duck first," Dad explained. "It's lots of fun. They have people dressed up as Disney cartoon characters."

"Aw," Laura complained. "I don't want to sound ungrateful, Mr. P, but that's little-kid stuff. I mean, meeting Donald Duck isn't on the top of my 'to do' list anymore. I'd rather go see Justin Adams."

"It's certainly not all for small children," Dad said. "We'll ride on Space Mountain. That's an indoor roller coaster. We'll visit the Haunted Mansion. I don't know how they do it, but the ghosts look real. There's even a scary alien ride. I bet you'll scream when the monster breathes on your neck. How does that sound, Laura?"

Laura nodded reluctantly. "It'll be fun, I guess. But seeing Justin Adams will be more fun. We'll do that in the afternoon, right?"

Dad shook his head. "Afraid not. It'll take us a whole day to see The Magic Kingdom. We'll go to the studios on Wednesday."

"Wednesday?" Laura gasped. "That's two whole days from now."

Dad smiled at her. "It'll make it all the more fun to wait. Disney World is too big to do in one day. We'll do The Magic Kingdom today. Tomorrow, we'll visit Epcot Center. On Wednesday, we'll visit Disney/MGM Studios. On Thursday, we'll go to Typhoon Lagoon and Blizzard Beach, which are huge water parks. And on Friday, we'll go back to whatever you liked the best."

Laura's face dropped into a massive frown. "I was just so psyched to see Justin Adams today. I've been dreaming about seeing him ever since Britt invited me along. I hardly slept at all last night. I'd close my eyes and I'd see his cute face smiling at me. We couldn't change the order, huh? Go to the Studios today and come back to Mickey Mouse land on Wednesday?"

"Sorry," Dad said. "The monorail doesn't go there. And it's a different parking lot. We'll stay in The Magic Kingdom today."

Laura's long face dropped some more.

Then Dad turned his attention to me. "You haven't said anything, Brittany."

"If you want to know the truth, I agree with Laura," I told him. "I'd rather go to the Studios first, but I understand what you're saying."

"You do?"

He didn't have to sound so surprised.

"You're the adult in charge," I went on. "You decide what's best."

He bit his bottom lip and studied me for a few seconds.

"I know I'm going to get to go to the Studios eventually," I added. "I can be patient."

There, that sounded like a mature statement. Truth was, I was almost as disappointed as Laura, but I couldn't act it. It was important that I follow the plan I'd thought up in bed last night. If I could show Dad I wasn't a little kid, he'd have to treat me differently.

I'd been polite since getting up. I hadn't put on any make-up. I was doing my best to stand up straight. I was trying my hardest to impress him.

"Hmm, I'll tell you what," Dad said. "How about we visit the Studios tomorrow instead of Wednesday? Is that a fair compromise?"

"I guess," Laura mumbled, less than enthusiastically. "If I've waited this long, I suppose I can wait another day."

"That sounds fine to me," I agreed.

"Good," Dad said. "Now let's catch the monorail."

The monorail took a couple of minutes to cross the river.

Laura bounced back from her disappointment quickly. By the time we got off at the gates of The Magic Kingdom, her braces had reappeared.

To enter the theme park, the crowd was funneled through Main Street, USA, a row of souvenir boutiques.

"They make sure you pass by the stores on the way in and out," Dad said. "I guess that's how they sell souvenirs."

"How come you know so much about Disney World, Mr. P?" Laura asked.

"Yeah, Dad," I wondered. "I didn't know you'd been here before."

He made a noise that sounded something like a nervous chuckle. "Didn't I tell you? I was here last summer."

"You didn't say anything about it on the phone," I told him. "Or in your letters."

"Guess I must have forgotten," he apologized.

Forgotten? How could anyone forget coming here? Something was fishy here. "Did you come alone?" I asked.

"Not really."

"What does that mean, Dad? Either you did or you didn't."

"What's with the third degree?" He made the funny chuckling noise again.

"Who'd you come with?" I probed.

"Sheila," he said. "My friend, Sheila."

"Does this Sheila own the condo we're staying in?" I asked.

He nodded.

"She's your girlfriend?" I went on.

"I suppose you could call her that," he answered.

"Then how come you didn't tell me about her? Where is she now?"

"She's in Chicago on a business trip."
Then he directed Laura and me off the
street into the doorway of one of the stores.
"Brittany, this is my personal life. I don't
feel comfortable discussing my personal life
with little children."

With little children, I thought. "I am
not . . ." I began, then quickly stopped. "Cool
it, Britt," I said to myself.

"Dad," I began as politely as I could. "I'm
your daughter. I'm curious, that's all."

"This is my personal life, Brittany.
Adults need some privacy. Why are you
being so nosy anyway?"

"I'm not being nosy, Dad," I tried to
explain. "I want to know what my father is
doing, just like you want to know what I'm
doing."

"I feel awkward discussing my private
life with a child," Dad confessed.

I forced myself to keep control.

"You shouldn't feel that way," Laura
blurted. "Britt knows all about the private
life of her Mom. She's been seeing this guy,
Kevin, for eight months. When Kevin visits
and he leaves they kiss for . . . " She stopped
when she saw me tugging frantically at my
earring. "Sorry," she mouthed to me.

The mention of my mother seemed to

make Dad more uptight. "I do not want to talk about this right now or right here."

I wasn't going to argue with that. Disney World was the last place to be discussing my father's love life. In spite of my curiosity to find out more about Sheila, and my anger that Dad considered me a "young child," I nodded in agreement.

We continued to stroll down the street.

"Let's go to Space Mountain first," Dad decided. "And before we go any further, we need to establish a few rules. Disney World is a large place and we might become separated."

"You mean get lost?" Laura asked.

"Exactly," Dad said.

"I get lost a lot," Laura admitted.

"I'm not surprised," Dad said, almost sarcastically. "Anyway, in the event that we *do* get separated, I want you to go to the last ride or building we went in together and wait by the entrance. And if you're suspicious about anything or anyone while we're separated, then immediately inform a security guard. Do you understand?"

We both nodded.

He reached out and mussed my hair again. Than he did the same to Laura. "Good girls."

I wanted to shout, "Don't do that!" but I swallowed my words. Getting into another argument wasn't going to impress my father. If we were going to have fun today and if I wanted him to change his opinion about me, I'd better shut up.

Trouble was, I didn't know how long I could keep my cool.

Chapter Eight

You Kiss Your Pillow?

Laura and I swam in the deep end of the condo pool while my dad sat on a deck chair by the shallow end. His face was buried in a *USA Today*.

We'd had lots of fun in The Magic Kingdom. The indoor roller coaster was awesome. In fact, Laura and I braved another half hour lineup to go on it a second time. The Haunted Mansion was equally super. I figured out the ghosts were just projections on a piece of glass. Laura agreed, but Dad thought there had to be something more complicated than that. And Splash Mountain was everything Dad said it would be. Ditto on the pirate boat ride. The best was when the ship fell down a waterfall.

We even enjoyed the parade of Disney cartoon characters in the afternoon. It was aimed at the little kids, but it sure was entertaining.

But that was the only little-kid thing I liked. I certainly didn't appreciate the way my father continued to treat me like a baby. He was constantly checking to see if I was still behind him in the line-ups. If we walked in a crowd, I had to hold his hand. He kept asking me if I was hungry or thirsty or had to go to the bathroom, as if I didn't know enough to tell him on my own.

I almost lost my temper a couple of times, but stuck to my plan. I took it all without saying a word, which was no easy chore.

Laura pulled herself out of the pool and sat on the edge. "You okay? You're not still spooked by that Alien Encounter ride, are you?"

"I'm fine," I said as I treaded water. "The monster didn't scare me. Honest.

"But you're so quiet. You're not sulking, but you're still real quiet."

I swam to the ladder, climbed out, wrapped myself in a beach towel and sat on a chair, as far away from my father as possible. A few moments later, Laura joined me.

"Are you going to answer my question or not?" she asked as she sat beside me.

"It's not as cold tonight," I said. "There's a warm breeze."

She sat back in her chair, twirled a wet curl around a finger and stared at me. "Let *me* tell *you* what's wrong then. It's what we talked about last night, isn't it? It's your dad and the way he's treating you. I noticed the look on your face every time he held your hand in the crowds."

"What am I going to do, Laura?"

"If it makes you feel any better, he held my hand a few times too."

I sighed. "It's not that I don't want my dad worrying about me. In a way, that's neat. It means he loves me. It's just that I'd like him to watch out for me when I need him to. I'm trying to pretend it doesn't bother me, but it's too much."

"Like I said yesterday, it has to be tough on your father only seeing you once a year. You have to talk to him. He needs to be told how you feel."

"This is my father," I scoffed. "There's no way he'd listen."

"My parents listen to me when I don't like something," she said. "Do you know they think I'm flaky?"

"Flaky?"

She tapped her forehead. "They think I'm a little thin in here."

"They do? Go figure."

"But they still listen to me. And I listen to them. Most of the time they tell me I'm full of it and they make me do what they want anyway. But sometimes they see my point of view, like when I told them I was useless at piano and never wanted to take another stupid plonk-plonk lesson as long as I lived."

I shook my head. "It will never work; my father is on a different wavelength."

"Are you two all right?" Dad called from the far side of the pool.

Laura flashed a thumbs-up.

He returned his attention to the newspaper.

"I really like talking to you, Laura. Telling you stuff makes me feel better."

"Me too. And I promise I won't blab it when we get back to Toronto. Speaking of parents, I felt major sympathy for most of the moms and dads lugging their little kids around The Magic Kingdom today."

"Why?"

"The way I see it, they probably saved for the trip for a couple of years," she explained. "They paid for plane tickets, hotel rooms, admission. They got their kids hyper about seeing Mickey and Donald and Goofy and everybody. They came here and it's so much fun that their five-year-old burned out by noon. The rest of the day they've got a wiped kid to amuse."

"I saw a few screamers," I said. "But on the whole, everybody seemed to be having a good time."

"Maybe you're right," she said. "Maybe I'm too good at spotting clones of my baby brother. I can smell a brat from way off."

I began a mighty yawn. "Excuse me," I said several seconds later. "I don't know about the five-year-olds, but I'm exhausted. How about you?"

"Dead beat," she nodded. "But there's no way I'm going to get much sleep tonight. I'll close my eyes and there will be Justin Adams smiling at me. Just think, Britt, tomorrow is the day. We're actually going to see the cutest boy in the universe."

"I sure hope so. I figure there's a good chance Justin Adams could be someplace else. And even if he is at the Studios, we may not get a chance to get close to him."

Laura shuddered. "Don't say that. Don't even think it. If you think it, it'll bring us bad luck. Do you think Justin has ever kissed a girl? For real, I mean, not like that girl on the show."

"How would I know ?"

"I don't think so," she said. "Wouldn't you like to be the first girl Justin Adams ever kisses?"

"I . . . I've never ever thought about it."

"I do. Every night. I practice kissing my pillow. I imagine my pillow is Justin and I kiss it."

"You kiss your pillow."

"Over and over, until I fall asleep."

"You kiss your *pillow*?"

"Don't look at me like I'm crazy," she scolded. "I'm practicing. You never can tell, someday Justin Adams might walk up to me and say, 'Hey, do you want to kiss?' If he ever does that, I have to be ready. Wouldn't that be the greatest thing that ever happened to you? Justin kissing you, then whispering in your ear, 'Do you want fries with that?' How scrumptious a thought. Maybe you should start kissing your pillow, Britt."

"I . . . Laura, I like you. You make me happy."

"What are friends for?" she replied.

Chapter Nine

Full Scream Ahead

We took another four-lane highway to get to the Disney/MGM Studios the next morning. We'd grabbed breakfast at a McDonald's Drive Thru and we were early enough to park the car within walking distance of the front gate. Since we already had our passes, we were among the first visitors into the park.

"There's the information booth, Mr. P," Laura declared. "Let's go find out how we can get into the *Do You Want Fries With That?* set and watch them film."

Laura ran to the woman behind the counter. By the time Dad and I caught up, my friend was halfway through her explanation. " . . . and we need three tickets to get in and be part of the *Do You Want Fries With That?* studio audience."

"Do You Want Fries With That?" The woman flipped through a thick blue binder. *"Do You Want Fries With That?* Let me see. That's one of my daughter's favorite shows. She's about your age and watches it every week. I enjoy it too. When I can watch. Sometimes I work here in the evenings. It really upsets your life when you work at night."

"That's great," Laura said impatiently. "Where do we get tickets?"

The woman flipped pages more slowly. *"Do You Want Fries With That?* Ah, yes, here it is."

"All right," Laura jumped so high she brushed her hair on the canvas awning. "What did I tell you, Britt? We're going to be part of the audience."

Her happiness was contagious and we gave each other a high five, like football players do.

"All right," I echoed.

"I'm sorry," the woman went on. "There's no way you can see that show."

Laura twisted around and slapped her hands on the counter. "Whatdoyoumeanbythat? Ihavetosee . . . "

"Whoa," Dad interjected. "Nobody can understand you when you're talking that fast, Laura. Slow down."

Laura took a deep breath and swallowed. "I didn't mean to act so hyper." She leaned closer to the woman and spoke only slightly slower. "You see, we *have* to see that show. It's a matter of life or . . . "

"Laura," Dad warned. "Let's not exaggerate."

"It's really important to us that we're part of the studio audience for that program," Laura pleaded.

The woman shook her head. "I am afraid that's impossible."

"Are all the tickets sold out?" I asked.

"No, it's not that," the woman explained. "There's no charge for seeing the productions. If there is a studio audience, it's on a first come, first served basis. I'm afraid that taping for *Do You Want Fries With That?* was finished last week. That was the last show of the season. They won't start taping new episodes until late August."

Laura made a hideous noise. She sounded like a bus had just run over her foot. "Eaargh!"

"I knew this was going to happen," I moaned. "I knew we shouldn't have got our hopes up."

Laura turned to me with wet eyes and a soggy expression.

Seeing her cry made me realize how awful *I* felt. "We'll still have fun," I said through my own near-tears.

She made the bus-over-the-foot noise again. "Eaargh."

Laura and I limply hugged each other.

"Are there any other TV shows in production?" Dad asked. "Would it be possible to see something else?"

The woman flipped through her binder again.

"I don't want to see anything else," Laura moaned. "My whole week is ruined. My whole life is ruined. I'll never smile again. I'm going to be miserable until I end up in an old folks' home with gray hair and a bald head."

"I think we're being a little over-dramatic, Laura," Dad observed.

"How can we have gray hair *and* a bald head?" I asked, sniffing a little.

Laura just groaned in my ear.

The woman continued to turn the pages in her binder.

"Yes, there is something today," she announced. "They're filming a spring special for the *Benny Bunny Fun Club*. That's a new show where kids sing and dance and do comedy skits."

"How about that, girls?" Dad tried his best to sound enthusiastic.

"No thanks, Mr. P," Laura continued to mope. "It was *Do You Want Fries With That?* or nothing. It was Justin Adams we wanted to see."

"Justin Adams?" the woman asked.

"I'm in love with him," Laura confessed. "I'm in love with his eyes."

"So is my daughter," the woman admitted. "She has posters of him all over her room. Want to hear a surprise?"

Laura shook her head. "I'm not in the mood for surprises. I'm just going to curl up and hibernate for the next fifty years."

"If you do that, you might miss Justin Adams," the woman said.

"What?" I asked.

"Whatdoyoumeanbythat?" Laura gasped at the same moment.

The woman smiled at my father. "According to this sheet, it says the two guest stars on the *Benny Bunny Fun Club Spring Special* are from *Do You Want Fries With That?*, Little Mike Davies and Justin Adams."

Laura glanced up at the sky. "Thank you. Thank you. Thank you," she whispered.

"Incredible," I said. "From the jaws of victory, we have snatched the agony of defeat." I thought for a second. "I mean, the other way around. Whatever."

Laura squealed and held up her thumb and forefinger. "We're this close to seeing Justin Adams."

"Will there be any problem getting in to see that?" Dad asked.

"There shouldn't be," the woman said. "I'll give you instructions on where to get passes. The taping doesn't start until one o'clock, so you'll have the entire morning to enjoy the rest of the park."

"A whole morning," Laura whined. "How am I supposed to survive a *whole* morning?"

Laura had a nervous fit when Dad couldn't locate the office that issued the passes for the studio audiences. Finally, he found the correct door and received three tickets from a security guard.

"Line up outside the gate marked Studio D at approximately 12:15," the guard instructed.

"Maybe we should get in line now," Laura reasoned. "We want to sit in the very first row, don't we?"

Dad checked his watch. "The show

doesn't begin for almost three hours. There'll be plenty of time to get a good seat. There's so many interesting things to see and do here."

"Still," Laura hedged. "Maybe you and Britt should go do those interesting things and leave me in line. I'll save your place."

"We'll all do interesting things," Dad said firmly. "When do you think you'll get a chance to be here again? You have to take advantage of it."

* * * * *

The Studios were great. I had a great time. Dad seemed impressed too, even though he was doing it for the second time. I wondered if he'd had as much fun with Sheila Condo-owner.

Laura obviously enjoyed everything too, but every ten minutes she asked my father what time it was. When he answered, she'd make comments like, "Only one hour and twenty-three minutes to Justin Adams."

Just before noon, we ate a quick lunch of pizza and Coke. Laura gorfed hers in thirty seconds. It took me only a little longer. We watched impatiently as Dad nibbled his way through his food. By the time we got to the entrance of Studio D, there was a handful of people waiting in line.

"How many chairs do you think there are in the front row?" Laura wanted to know.

"I'm sure we'll get a good seat," Dad assured her.

And we did, front row, a little to the left of center.

"This is completely too impossible to believe," Laura babbled. "We're going to be two meters from Justin Adams."

I thought seven was a better guess. There was so much going on between us and the painted stage. The studio was abuzz with technicians aiming lights, positioning cameras, adjusting sound booms and moving the set scenery of the *Benny Bunny Fun Club*.

"How come you're not going insane like me?" Laura wanted to know. "You look happy, but you're being so cool. I feel like I'm going to explode."

"I'm really excited," I told her. "I don't believe it's happening either."

"Well, act it then," Laura coached. "Act like your brain is floating in Alka-Seltzer. Bounce up and down like me."

"I think one of us doing that is enough," I said.

Actually, I was deliberately trying to

stay calm. I didn't want to start squealing and hyperventilating like Laura because of Dad. What would he think if I acted like a crazed teenybopper? It wouldn't stop him from treating me like a little kid, that's for sure.

A few minutes before one o'clock, a plump man with Benny Bunny ears came out and told us a few dopey jokes. Dad whispered in my ear that he was the "warm-up person" and it was his job to get the audience relaxed and in a good mood.

Then a middle-aged woman with a smile as wide as Laura's spoke to us. "My name is Karen," she began. "I'm the director. Just a few words before we begin. We want you to have a good time, but please stay seated throughout the taping. And please help us out by clapping when we light the applause signs directly above the front bank of lights. Let's try that now."

The applause signs began flashing and everyone clapped on cue.

"Thank you," Karen said. "Enjoy yourselves."

Laura grabbed the armrests of her seat the same way she'd done on the airplane. This time, though, she was trying to hold herself down, rather than hold the plane up.

I felt excitement run through my stomach and I needed a deep breath to settle down. There was a flourish of the *Benny Bunny Fun Club* theme music through the speakers and a half dozen BunnyKids appeared and performed a lively one-minute dance number. We could watch what the people at home would see on the monitors suspended next to the applause signs. As the music faded, one of the cameras moved into a close-up on two of the BunnyKids.

"Well, Wendy," the boy said. "We have a wonderful special show for everyone out there. There are guaranteed to be lots of surprises."

"That's right, Brad," Wendy replied to the camera. "And I'd like to introduce two of them right away . . . our guest stars from that popular TV show, *Do You Want Fries With That?,* Little Mike Davies . . . "

The applause signs flashed and we clapped as the little guy came running in from the left side of the stage. He shook hands with Wendy and Brad. I couldn't help thinking he was just as cute in real life as on TV. If I had a little brother, I'd want him to be like Little Mike.

Wendy returned her attention to the camera. " . . . and Justin Adams."

Again the applause signs blinked and again we applauded. Laura and I clapped extra loud. Justin jogged in from the right side of the stage. And like Little Mike, Justin was cute. No, that's no true, he was majorly cuter. Majorly. His sandy hair was a little longer than on *Do You Want Fries With That?* and it waved on his shoulders. He turned to the audience and smiled. I figured it had to be impossible to look at those gorgeous eyes and *not* dissolve away.

My appreciation of Justin's good looks was interrupted by a piercing screech beside me. It was Laura pulling on her hair and screaming, "Justin! Justin! Justin! I love you, Justin!"

I reached over and shook her arm. "Laura," I said. "Stop it."

She ignored me and bolted from her chair. She ran, full scream ahead, through the cameras and booms and wires.

Directly toward Justin Adams.

Chapter Ten

Justin Adams

I've never seen my father move as fast as he did then. He was on his feet a fraction of a second behind Laura. By the time she reached the cameras, he'd caught up with her and grabbed the back of her T-shirt to stop her. He gently but firmly pulled her back to her seat.

"Justin!" Laura screamed hysterically. "Justin!"

"Cut!" Karen, the director, called from somewhere behind the lights. "Cut the tape."

Laura was a mess of flailing arms and legs. She fought against Dad's grip, but he reeled her slowly back into her seat.

"Justin!" she continued to scream. "I love you, Justin!"

I noticed Justin Adams watching the

chaos. He seemed so calm, so cool, as if this sort of thing happened all the time.

Maybe it did. There had to be thousands of girls in the world who felt the same way about him as Laura and I did. Maybe even millions of girls?

"Laura, stop it, right now." Dad flashed his full demon face. His scalp shone with beady sweat, his eyes got wide and white and a web of throbbing veins covered his head. "Stop it," he commanded.

Laura, in mid-screech, glanced up at him and was suitably intimidated. She instantly stopped screaming. It was like she'd been on another planet and had suddenly been transported back to the Starship Enterprise. "Oh, no," she muttered. "I'm sorry, Mr. P. Something just sort of took me over. I don't know why I did that."

Karen appeared beside Dad. "I'm sorry, sir, but the girl will have to leave."

"I beg your pardon? Why will that be necessary?" Dad asked.

"No," Laura protested with a loud whine. "Don't kick me out. I've waited my whole life for this moment."

"Let her stay," I pleaded.

"I can't have any more interruptions," Karen explained to my father. "I can't have my performers threatened like that."

"Threatened?" Dad said. "I hardly think that's the correct word."

A security guard appeared behind Dad. "This way, sir."

"Do something, Dad," I coached.

"Just a moment." My father pointed at Laura. "This young lady is a fan of Justin Adams. The reason Justin Adams is so popular is because of his fans. If they didn't feel for him the same way she does, then I imagine Justin Adams would be going to a normal seventh grade class and doing normal seventh grade things. The fact that Justin Adams is a special person is because of the many, many girls exactly like her."

"And me," I added.

Then it dawned on me what was happening. Dad was sticking up for Laura. He wasn't angry at her. He wasn't embarrassed by the fact that a hundred people in the studio audience and two dozen BunnyKids and technicians were watching him. It was incredible.

"Justin Adams is in eighth grade," Laura said meekly.

Dad continued. "For a moment, this girl was temporarily overcome by being so close to a person she admires very much. I'm sure you can understand that, Karen. You are in the entertainment business. You know how important it is to have people interested in your stars. You have our promise it will not happen again."

"This way, sir," the security guard puffed out his chest.

"Please, Karen," Dad finished his plea bargain. "You have our word this incident won't be repeated. Isn't that correct, Laura?"

"Oh yes, yes," my friend pledged. "I don't know why I did it. I was just so excited. I won't do it again. Please let me stay. Pretty please with a . . . Please don't kick me out."

Karen's eyes flicked from my father to Laura, then to the control booth, to the security guard, to me, over at Justin Adams and back to Laura.

"Let her stay," Justin called from the stage. "It's no big deal. We can pick it up from my intro."

Karen didn't say anything for a few moments. Finally, "All right. I expect you to keep your promise," she said sternly to Laura.

"I will. I will. Thank you, ma'am."

And if my father's behavior wasn't surprising enough, another incredible thing happened. The audience began to clap, even though the applause sign wasn't on. They were applauding for my friend, cheering for Laura. They were pleased with the way things had turned out. It was almost like they were saying they understood why she'd acted so bizarre.

Laura and I grinned at each other.

"Just imagine," I whispered to Laura. "Justin Adams pitched in for you. A TV superstar, the pin-up of half the girls in our homeroom, half the girls in North America, stood up for you. Wait until I tell Lucy-Mae Bennett."

"Don't tell anybody, okay?" she whispered back.

"Why not?" I wondered.

"I'll die of embarrassment if you tell the kids at school how I tried to attack Justin Adams."

"Some things I'll never understand."

Karen was looking at the control booth. "Let's pick it up after Justin's intro."

The applause sign flashed and the show rolled.

Like everything else we'd seen in the last two days, the *Benny Bunny Fun Club Spring Special* was exciting and entertaining. There were lots of songs and comedy skits. Justin Adams didn't have all that much to do with it. He did have a skit where he played an overweight Easter Bunny. It's no use me describing it; you'll have to see it.

Little Mike Davies stole the show. Every time he mugged at the camera the crowd began to cheer. They didn't need prompting by the sign.

The grand finale of the show featured all the BunnyKids dancing. They even yanked a few people from the audience. I was hoping they'd pick me, so I could get even closer to Justin Adams. They didn't.

They didn't pick Laura either. She looked crestfallen. She'd been sitting on the edge of her seat throughout the whole performance. And every time Justin Adams appeared, she leaned a little bit closer.

Finally, the bright lights dimmed, the actors left the stage and the technicians began to pack up the wires and equipment. Karen thanked us for our co-operation and told us to leave by the exit at the back.

As we stood up, she approached Laura. "Thank you for behaving yourself. You know, I *do* understand your feelings. When I was younger, I had a crush on The New Kids on the Block."

"Who are they?" Laura asked.

Karen frowned at my father. "I guess I must be older than I thought."

"How old *are* you?" Laura asked.

I gave her a quick elbow and tugged on my earring.

"You look so young to be such an important person," Laura recovered quickly.

"Thanks for being so understanding," Dad said.

"You're welcome. I hope you enjoyed the show and you'll watch it on TV in a couple of weeks." Karen nodded her head good-bye and walked toward the control booth.

"I'm real sorry about what happened at the beginning, Mr. P," Laura apologized. "I didn't mean to get that excited. It was real dumb of me. Sorry I embarrassed you."

"I wasn't embarrassed, Laura," Dad said. "I'm just glad we were allowed to stay."

Laura bobbed her head. "Me too. Now I can be happy for the rest of my life. I actually got to see Justin Adams in person. All the girls at school are going to be so jealous of me."

"Of us," I added. "I was there too."

"Yeah, but Justin wasn't looking at you throughout the whole performance," Laura said. "He was looking at me."

"How could you tell that?" I wondered. "He was only on for a few minutes and he was wearing a bunny mask."

"I could tell," Laura boasted. "It's female instinction."

"I think you mean female intuition," Dad corrected.

"Whatever," Laura said. "I could sense it."

And speaking of intuition, I suddenly got a strange feeling. I had the feeling Laura and I were going to meet Justin Adams again.

"What were you just thinking of, Britt?" Laura asked. "You looked real spacey for a second."

I shrugged. "Nothing really. Just thinking about Justin."

Chapter Eleven

Enough Is Enough

"Let's go and see how they make special effects," Dad suggested when got back outside. "You'll learn how they make monsters. There's a fascinating show."

"I'd rather go for a walk down the fake old western street," I said. "I want to go see where they filmed *The Young Outlaws*."

"We'll do that after." Dad pointed at the brightly painted building sporting the name Movie Miracles. "First, we'll go see the show. It only lasts about twenty minutes."

"What if you go see the show and Laura and I go for the walk? I really want to do something outside in the sunshine."

"I don't know, Britt," Laura confessed. "I think I'd rather go see the special effects show. That sounds really special."

Dad laughed. "That's funny, Laura. The special effects show is *special*."

Laura and I smiled weakly at the joke.

"Okay," I said. "Tell you what. I'll go for the walk and you guys go to the show."

Dad shook his head. "Absolutely not. We'll all go to the show."

"Why?" I protested. "I want to do something outside."

"Don't start acting like a spoiled child, Brittany," Dad scolded. "I heard what you want to do and I said we're going to the special effects presentation."

I felt the back of my neck get hot and once again it was an effort to keep my voice under control. "A spoiled child? That's not fair, Dad. What's wrong with me doing one thing and you doing another? I'll meet you back here in half an hour."

"I am not going to let you wander for a half hour when I don't know where you are," Dad lectured. "Anything could happen to you."

"Like what?" I asked.

There was a hint of sweat on Dad's scalp. "Many things," he said bluntly.

"Like what?" I repeated. "There's hundreds of people everywhere you turn. There's security guards all over the place.

What's going to happen to me with all those people around?"

Veins appeared on his temples. "Brittany, you may believe that you are old enough to wander around by yourself, but you have a lot to learn about people. You may look grown up, but you are still a little girl and it's my responsibility to watch out for you."

Little girl? *Okay, enough is enough*, I thought. There is only so much of this . . . you know . . . this garbage I could take.

"I'm not stupid," I said angrily. "Mom trusts me. She lets me ride the subway by myself to go shopping downtown in the daytime."

He was surprised by that. "Your mother lets you go downtown alone? I'll have to talk to her about that."

"I promise not to take candy from a stranger," I said in a little-kid voice.

"Don't get sarcastic with me," Dad snarled. "The answer is no. You may not go off alone. You will come to the special effects show with Laura and me."

"I don't want to go," I snarked back. So much for my plan of being obedient and polite. I had to stand up to my father. Now it was a matter of principle. I'd show him I wasn't a little kid by holding firm. "Are you going to make me?"

Laura seemed about to say something, so I tugged on my earring. This was between my father and me.

"You are not going to spoil my enjoyment or Laura's," Dad threatened. "You will come with us or you will sit there until we are finished." He pointed to a bench just outside the Movie Miracles building and right next to an information booth occupied by a security guard.

"You'd let little me wait by myself for a whole half hour? Who knows what might happen to me?" I mocked. "I could get hit by lightning. I could get swallowed by an earthquake."

"You could get eaten by an alligator," Laura volunteered. "Or attacked by a swarm of fruit flies with rabies."

I gave her a what-are-you-talking-about expression. Dad just ignored her.

I expected my father to get super angry, to make an all-out demon face. Maybe I wanted that. I wanted to get mad too. I certainly didn't want the "little-kid" deal any more. Instead, he wiped a handkerchief over his scalp and pointed at the bench. "Wait there, Brittany. Laura and I will be out shortly. You can be miserable all by yourself."

"Great," I snapped. "It's better than being with you."

That, too, failed to make him angry. Maybe he was saving it up so he could dump on me later. "You will not move from that bench," he ordered. "I want you sitting within sight of that security guard the entire time we're inside."

Laura gave me a sympathetic look. Another tug on my earlobe stopped her from offering her opinion. I stomped over to the bench, sat down, folded my arms across my chest and glared at my father.

He glared back for a few seconds before walking over to the security guard and speaking to her. The guard looked at me and nodded. Dad returned to Laura and directed her into the entrance of the Movie Miracles building.

I brooded for a couple of minutes. Then I noticed a family asking the security guard for information. They were blocking her view of me, so I stood up and strolled over to a T-shirt shop. Even if I couldn't go for a walk on the old western street, I wasn't going to be a good little girl.

I began to check out the pink, green and

white T-shirts sporting various Disney World logos and landmarks. I spent a few minutes browsing, holding up one shirt after another and wondering out loud which would look best.

Then I heard a familiar voice behind me. "I like the green one."

At first, I thought I was imagining it. I'd heard that voice many, many times before. But I shouldn't be hearing it in a souvenir store. This was definitely the wrong place. The voice belonged on TV.

"You'd look good in the pink, too," the voice went on.

It had to be. There was no doubt about it. Justin Adams was talking to me.

Chapter Twelve

More Justin Adams

Justin Adams was talking to me?

I spun around to find the source of the voice. It was Justin Adams. But it wasn't him. The boy looked like Justin Adams. But there was something wrong with the picture. It was the hair. The boy I was staring at had long, dark hair.

"It's a wig," the boy answered my unasked question. "I borrowed it from the wardrobe department. I wear it when I sneak out."

"You're Ju . . . Justin Ad . . . Ad . . . Adams," I stuttered.

He smiled. "I saw you in the studio earlier. You were sitting with the girl who ran on the stage. She sure was excited. "

"Jus . . . tin Ad . . . Adams," I muttered. "You're him."

"I hope you don't think I'm rude just coming up and talking to you when I don't know you," he went on.

I actually pinched the back of my hand. This couldn't be happening. Justin Adams wasn't really talking to me, wearing a black wig, in the middle of a souvenir T-shirt shop. This couldn't be happening. It was impossible.

"Can we talk for a couple of minutes?" Justin asked.

"What are . . . why are you . . . you're Justin Adams."

"Don't look so stunned. It's me." He looked concerned. "You're not going to scream like your friend, are you? You're not going to give me away?"

I shook my head too quickly, making myself a little dizzy. "No, Laura and I are very different in all sorts of ways even though we're best friends for only eight weeks you're Justin Adams."

He laughed. "I think I understood that. Do you have a few minutes to talk?"

Again, I nodded my head too quickly. The image of Justin Adams bounced in my sight for several seconds.

"Let's go sit on the bench and I'll buy you an ice cream," he suggested.

I walked dumbly back to the bench Dad had ordered me not to leave and watched Justin approach the ice cream vendor. "That's Justin Adams," I said to myself. "The boy whose posters cover my bedroom walls. The boy whose name is inside the giant heart on the front of my binder. The boy all the girls in my class would love to go to a dance with. Justin Adams is buying me ice cream. He's talking to me. Why does Justin Adams want to talk to me?"

Justin sat on the bench and handed me an ice cream bar. It was shaped like Mickey Mouse's head.

"You know," he began. "This is great. The fact you're talking to me, that is. I mean, it must seem weird to you. You don't know me or anything. Where's your friend?"

I swallowed to get my tongue to work properly. I told him about Dad and Laura and how I was waiting for them to come out of Movie Miracles.

"It's a good show," Justin told me. "I snuck in there once. They show how they made the slimeworms work in *I Spent My Summer Vacation Kidnapped Into Space*. You ever see that movie?"

I shook my head and bit off one of the ice cream bars ears. The shock of meeting him was wearing off . . . a little. My dumbfound-edness was slowly being replaced by . . . curiosity.

"What's your name and where are you from?" he asked.

I told him.

"Canada, huh? I've been there a couple of times. I don't remember much. Every time I visit someplace all I get to see is a hotel and a couple of shopping malls."

"How come you're out free and wearing a wig like that?" I asked.

"Out free," he mused. "That's about it. I'm out among real people for about ten minutes because being chained to my dressing room drives me nuts. I wear the wig as a disguise and so my chaperone, Sharon the Barbarian, will have a hard time if she comes looking for me. She's the one who makes my life tough."

"How come you have to do that? You're a star. You can do anything you want." I bit off the other ear.

He laughed. "Right. Tell me about it. Was that your father who talked to Karen in the studio?"

My mouth was full of ice cream so I nodded.

"He said something about me being a

normal person if it wasn't for the fans. Remember?"

I nodded again.

"Well, there are times I really wish I was living in some small town, riding my mountain bike to school, playing on a ball team, treating a girl to ice cream. Doing normal stuff."

That sounded incredible. "You'd rather do that than be a star?"

He nodded. "You know what it's like being a star?"

I thought that was a dumb question. How would I know anything about it?

"I'll tell you what it's like to be a *star*," he continued. "It's hard work. I get up at five o'clock to be in Make-Up for six. We start shooting at seven. I have to do three hours of schoolwork with a tutor every day. By the time we finish it's usually seven or eight at night. Then I have to go home and do homework or learn my lines for the next day. Sharon the Barbarian won't let me go out alone. She wants to 'protect me,' she says. I spend the whole day with adults. I have no friends. Oh, there's Little Mike, of course. He and I share a condo with Sharon. But I don't know anybody our age I can visit or call on the phone. Even when I'm with my folks in LA, there's nobody. Course, I'm only there a few weeks a year. *That's* how much fun it is to be a star."

"What about the girl who plays your girlfriend on *Do You Want Fries With That?* I asked. "You seem real close to her."

"Marlene Powell." He said the name in a less-than-friendly manner. "We're only close on TV. Marlene thinks she's going to be the greatest movie star in the world. She's so stuck-up she doesn't even speak to me outside of her lines."

I worked on devouring the mouse's face.

"Besides, she's sixteen."

"She's sixteen?" I mumbled through ice cream and chocolate. "She looks twelve."

"Make-up," he said matter-of-factly. "And you ever notice how all the clothes she wears are baggy? They do that on purpose to hide her . . . " He blushed slightly.

"Wow," I said. "I didn't know that."

Justin finished his ice cream and glanced at his watch. "Being a star is the pits. That's why I sometimes need to put on a wig and walk around like real people."

"Wow." As each second passed, I found it easier and easier to be sitting next to him. "Do you often start talking to people like you did with me?"

Justin shook his head. "No. To tell the truth, I was looking forward to spending some time with the actors who play the BunnyKids, but Sharon sent me to my dressing room. I'm shooting a promo spot for *Do You Want Fries With That?* in a few minutes. But I *had* to get out. When I saw you, I said to myself, 'She looks friendly. I'll bet she'll talk to me for a few minutes.' "

"I'm glad you did," I told him.

"Me too. You've got ice cream on your nose."

"I do?" I wiped frantically at my nose with my hand. Then I cringed. What a goof I was. I was talking to Justin Adams with ice cream on my nose.

"Don't be embarrassed," he said. "It was kind of cute. You're really . . . er . . . you're pretty."

For some reason that made me feel so uncomfortable I had to look away.

"Did I say something wrong?" Justin sounded worried. "Maybe I shouldn't have said that."

"It's all right," I told him. "It's just that no boy has ever said anything like that to me before."

He thumped the side of his head with the palm of his hand. "I'm sorry. I don't get much of a chance to talk to girls. The only time I do is when I'm acting and then somebody has written the lines for me."

"It's no problem," I said. "It was kind of nice."

His big blue eyes sparkled at me. "What do boys usually say to you?"

"Oh, the usual. 'Get out of the way, Dogbreath.' 'You smell, Pond Scum.' Stuff like that."

"You're putting me on."

"Not really," I said.

"If I was at your school and somebody said that to you, they'd have to answer to me."

"They would?"

He nodded. "Look, Brittany, I was wondering . . . "

"Call me Britt. All my friends do."

"Okay." Again his eyes flashed a smile. "I was wondering, Britt, could you give me your phone number?"

"My phone number?"

"You're so easy to talk to. I wouldn't mind calling you on the phone every once in a while."

"You want to phone me?"

"I want to be your friend."

I gulped the last of my ice cream. "You want to be friends with me?"

"Isn't this how it works?" he asked. "Do I sound stupid? Like I said, I'm not really good at this."

"I'd love to be your friend," I blurted. "I mean, I'd like to be your friend. I'd like that a lot."

Part of my brain was screaming just like Laura, "Justin! Justin!" Justin Adams had just asked me to be his friend.

Chapter Thirteen

The Secret

"You must think I'm nuts," Justin said, "just walking up to you and asking if I can be your friend. It is kind of weird. But you don't know how lonely it is in there." He gestured toward the studio building.

"Yeah, it's weird," I agreed. "I mean, if you were a regular person it would be weird, but what makes it weirder is you're Justin Adams. You're famous. Everybody in the whole world knows you, except for Susan, the flight attendant."

"Pardon?"

"It's not important. What I'm trying to say, Justin," I paused, feeling awkward using his name for the first time. "What you have to understand is, I'm used to seeing your face in magazines. On posters on my wall. You and me sitting on a bench in the middle of Disney World is something . . . it's so incredible. You're a superstar."

He made an "aw shucks" expression. "Sometimes I forget what a good job the publicity department does. But I'm just a normal, average, everyday superstar."

I laughed. "That makes a lot of sense."

I went over to the security guard, borrowed a pen, begged a napkin from the ice cream vendor and wrote down my name and phone number on it.

He took it from me and shoved it into his shirt pocket. "Thanks. I won't bother you that often."

"Anytime," I said.

Justin tapped his watch with a finger. "I have to get going," he told me. "If I'm late for the promo, Sharon the Barbarian will have a fit."

"Say, you can't wait another couple of minutes, can you? Laura would simply melt at the chance to meet you. Besides she won't believe me when I tell her you bought me an ice cream and you're going to phone and . . . and . . . she just won't believe it."

"Sorry, I really have to go," he said as he stood up. Then he snapped his fingers. "Say, why don't you get your father to drive you and Laura to the condo where Little Mike and I are staying. It's got a pool. You guys could come for a swim after supper. You'll like Little Mike. He's just like on TV. He doesn't act; he's just himself."

"What about your chaperone?"

"No problem. The shooting is all finished today. I'm flying home to LA tomorrow. No lines to memorize tonight. No homework. I'm owed a little time off. What do you say?"

I couldn't hide my smile. "I'm sure that'll be terrific. Laura will go completely snaky."

"She won't chase me, will she?" he asked cautiously.

"My dad will tie her down."

"All right then. You guys can help me teach Little Mike to swim. He's turning into a real water rat. Come over any time after supper. We're not too far away from here. We're in Orlando. My manager has rented this weird condo. You'll have no trouble finding it. It looks like something from *Star Trek*. It's called . . . "

"Emerald Place?"

"How'd you know that?"

"You're not going to believe this . . . " I began.

I hastily explained about my father's

mysterious girlfriend and how we were staying at her place.

"Isn't that just too crazy?" I finished. "You were staying so close to us. I was sleeping right next to you." I thought for a minute. "I mean, I wasn't sleeping *next* to you. We were just close, like near each other in close buildings . . . like not really . . . "

Justin pretended not to notice my embarrassment. "Why don't you surprise Laura? I'll bet it'll blow her away when Little Mike and I show up at the pool."

"I don't think I can keep it a secret," I confessed.

"It's up to you," he said. "I have to go before Sharon sends a SWAT team to find me." And with that, he jogged into the crowd.

I returned the security guard's pen and waited for Dad and Laura to return. A few minutes later, the doors of Movie Miracles opened and a flood of people poured down the steps. Dad approached me with a wary look, as if he was ready to pick up our argument. Laura, on the other hand, was showing an enthusiastic mouthful of orthodontic artistry.

"I'm not going to tell them," I said to myself. "I'm going to do my best to keep it a secret."

"That was awesome, Britt," Laura said. "They showed us how they fake gun shots and how they make monsters move. They even had — "

"Slimeworms from the movie, *I Spent My Summer Vacation Kidnapped Into Space*," I said.

"Yeah, how'd you know?" she asked.

"I've heard about it."

"It was great," she finished. "You really missed something."

And so did you, I thought.

"I'm glad you liked it," I said.

"Are you feeling any better?" my father wanted to know.

"Do you mean, am I still mad? No, I'm fine now," I told him.

"What did you do while we were inside, Brittany?" Dad asked.

I had an ice cream with Justin Adams, is what I wanted to scream. "Waited for you," is what I said.

Dad waved a thank-you to the security guard. "Let's go check out the old western street now," he said to us.

The crowd flowing from the stunt show surrounded us, and we were forced to move slowly through the mass of people. Dad reached back to take my hand.

110

"What are you so happy about?" Laura asked me as we jostled among the herd of humans. "You're so bouncy-like. I thought you'd still be upset at your dad."

I had to tell her something. There was no way I could keep it inside for the rest of the afternoon.

"I met a boy," I told her.

"You what?"

"I met a boy," I repeated.

"You met a boy?" she gasped.

"Shussh." I pointed at my father, in front of me.

"How did you met him?" Laura asked.

"He bought me ice cream and sat next to me on the bench," I said.

"He bought you ice cream? A boy did that? He sat next to you? Tell me more."

"He saw me in the TV audience."

"No kidding." She scrunched her face. "Was he cute? You must have really liked him. You're sort of glowing."

"Glowing?"

Dad glanced briefly at us. "Everything okay?"

We nodded.

As soon as Dad turned forward, Laura poked me in the ribs. "Where is he now? What happened to him?"

"He had to go do something."

She slapped my arm. "You're being so mysterious. Some strange boy comes up to you and buys you ice cream and makes you all glowy and you don't want to tell me about it. Where's he from? Are you going to meet him again?"

We're both going to meet him again, I thought. "He's from around here," I told her. "But I gave him my phone number and he's going to call me."

"Call you?" Laura exclaimed. "You gave a strange boy your phone number? Maybe that wasn't a smart thing to do. What if he's a weirdo or something?"

Dad glanced around again. "What are you two talking about?"

"Nothing, Dad. Just about Disney World." In a way that wasn't a lie.

"I have to go to the toilet, Mr. P," Laura said quickly. "And so does Britt."

Dad nodded. "I could use a rest stop as well." That was his way of saying he had to go too.

He let go of my hand and we eased off to the right, heading into our respective bathrooms. I opened a stall door, but Laura closed it again and tugged me toward the sinks.

"I thought you had to go," I said.

She winked at me. "Of course I don't. I want to hear about this boy. This boy you like so much you gave him your phone number after knowing him for a few minutes."

"He was easy to talk to," I said.

"What was so special about him? He must have been really cute. Come on, Britt. Open up. This is really exciting."

I took my pik from the back pocket of my shorts and puffed my hair.

"Your hair is perfect. It always is. Stop being so . . . tell me. How old is he? Is he cute?"

"Thirteen. And he's definitely cute," I said. "A lot like Justin Adams."

"Like Justin Adams," she swooned. "No wonder you're glowing."

"Only he had dark hair," I went on.

"Dark hair is good too," she reasoned. "Just being like Justin Adams is enough. I wish I could get to meet him."

"I think you will," I told her. "He lives near us in Orlando. He said he could come over and go swimming tonight. And he's going to bring a friend."

"Really?" She clapped her hands together. "What a great vacation. First we get to see Justin Adams and now you fall in love."

"Get serious." I laughed.

"Is his friend cute?" she wanted to know.

"So I hear."

"Ewww, how exciting."

"You're right. It is," I agreed. "And I believe in intuition."

"Huh?"

"You know, female instinction."

"Huh?"

"I'll tell you later."

Now that I'd told her Laura my secret, I was having a wonderful time keeping the other half from her. She'd be so surprised, so shocked, when she found out who the boy was.

Laura was right — it had turned out to be a great vacation. Meeting a normal, average, everyday superstar. Who would have thought?

And who would have thought what the next few hours would bring?

Chapter Fourteen

A Red Sports Car

The old western movie street was fake, just the fronts of buildings, but unless you peered through the windows you'd swear it was all real. At the end of the street was a huge painting of the mountains. From where we stood it seemed like you were gazing across a cactus-covered desert at real mountains.

After we marveled at the movie make-believe for an hour, Dad treated Laura and me to a souvenir. We had our pictures put on magazine covers. Like the street, they looked like the genuine article. The magazine I choose was *Teen Gossip*. The title under my photo read, *Sexy Teen Singer Tells All Her Secrets*.

Dad commented. "That's almost in bad taste."

Laura had her photo placed on the cover of *Tattle Tale* magazine. Under her picture it said, *Psychic Reveals Elvis Was An Alien*.

We took three trips on the *Star Wars* ride, left the theme park, ate in a Dennys in Orlando and returned to Sheila Whoever's condo as it was getting dark. By that time, I was bursting to let Laura in on my secret. I was amazed that I'd held it in all day.

The pool was empty. I checked the strange windows of the other condos hoping to see Justin Adams or Little Mike Davies looking out for us. All I saw were drapes and blinds. I wondered which house the stars of *Do You Want Fries With That?* were sharing with their chaperone.

"We're going to go swimming," I told Dad.

"No, you're not," he said. "Not for another half hour. You don't go in the water right after you've eaten. I'm going to shave. When I'm finished, we'll all go down."

Laura and I watched MTV while we waited for Dad.

"You know, I'm still all tingly about seeing Justin Adams," Laura gushed. "There's part of me that still doesn't believe it." She stretched out her arms. "We were this close to Justin. It's so sad, isn't it?"

"Sad?"

"We'll probably never, ever see him again. Isn't that an awful thought?"

"I wouldn't bet on it." I tried to sound as casual as possible. "Who knows what could happen? We could meet him anywhere, at any time."

"Right," she grumbled. "Fat chance. In a few days, we'll be back in Toronto and he'll be here."

"You can never tell what could happen." I was sure the excitement in my voice would give me away. But Laura didn't catch on.

"Stop trying to be so positive, Britt. You sound like Lucy-Mae. Let's talk about something less depressing. When are those boys going to come over?"

"They said after supper."

"Maybe we should go down and wait by the pool. What if they show up and we're not there and they go away?"

"We'll meet them," I assured her. But I had a sudden jolt of anxiety. What if something went wrong with the commercial Justin was shooting? What if he had to stay at the studio until it was really late? Too late to go swimming?

"Do you think I should put on some make-up, Britt?"

"Why?"

"Because. You think I should cover my freckles?"

"I really like your freckles."

"Sure," she said. "But you're you. You're not a cute boy."

"Thank goodness for that," I declared. "Don't hide the freckles."

"Why did the teenager cross the road?"

"What?"

"It's a joke," Laura said. "Why did the teenager cross the road?"

"What has that got to do with freckles?"

"Nothing. It's a joke. Why did the teenager cross the road?"

I shrugged. "I don't know. Why did the teenager cross the road?"

"Because somebody told him not to," she said. "That's funny, huh? Because somebody told him *not* to."

"It's slightly amusing."

"It's slightly amusing," she imitated. "It's *funny*. What do you think you're going to be like as a teenager?"

"Like I said, when I'm talking to you, it's like riding on Space Mountain. Up, down. Around and around."

"So what do you think you'll be like when you're sixteen?"

"I haven't really thought about it. Like I am now, I guess."

"That'll be boring, won't it?" Laura blurted. "Let's hope you won't be like you are now when you're sixteen. Sixteen. It sounds so neat, doesn't it? What kind of car do you think you'll buy?"

"You think I'm boring?" I asked.

"I'm going to buy something fast and red," Laura raved on. "Something that people will turn around to look at when I drive into the high school parking lot. I'm already saving to buy it. I've saved thirty-eight dollars so far."

"I'm boring?"

Laura smiled. "I don't really mean it. I'm teasing."

"You know, I'm going to have to learn to ignore a lot of the stuff you say," I told her.

She laughed. "So what do you think of my car? Red? I was also thinking about black. It's sexier, isn't it?"

"You won't be able to buy a sports car when you're sixteen," I said. "They cost a lot of money. I'll bet the cheapest one is twenty thousand dollars."

"I'll get a job at the Burger King after school," she reasoned.

"At five dollars an hour? You know how

long it would take to save twenty thousand?"

"Not that long," Laura began to work out the math on her fingers. "Let's see. Suppose I work ten hours a week after school; that's fifty dollars a week. If I save fifty dollars a week . . . "

"You'll spend some," I interrupted. "You won't save it all."

"Okay, suppose I save half of it. I'll save twenty-five dollars a week. That's a hundred dollars a month. I'll save twelve hundred a year. That means I'll have my car in . . . " She worked her fingers. " . . . oh, no, that's almost seventeen years. I'll be over thirty before I can afford my sweet sixteen sports car."

"It could be worse," I said as I quickly worked out my own math problem in my head. "If you were a fruit fly you'd have been dead for forty thousand fruit-fly-years."

I don't think I've ever laughed as hard as I did for the next few minutes. My laughter came out in a machine gun of chuckles. My stomach hurt so much I thought I was going to throw up. Laura was in a similar condition. She laughed so much that she slipped off the chair and fell in a heap on the floor, gasping.

We'd only partially recovered by the time my father came out of the bathroom.

"What are you two laughing about?" he asked. "It must be pretty funny."

"It is," Laura told him. "We're laughing about fruit flies."

And that started us up all over again.

* * * * *

After I changed into my swimsuit, I peeked through the venetian blinds at the swimming pool. To my delight, I could see two boys. The pool lights revealed a wet-haired Justin Adams kneeling by the side, watching his young co-star in the shallow end. Little Mike was thrashing his arms and legs in an attempt to swim.

I couldn't wait to talk to him again. And it was going to be such an outstanding surprise for Laura. I wondered what she would do. She might actually faint. Or start screaming again. I'd have to make sure I was standing close to her.

I slipped my T-shirt back on and grabbed a towel. Laura and Dad waited for me by the open patio doors.

"I'm glad you've finally settled down. Fruit flies?" Dad mumbled.

"The boys are there," I said to Laura.

Laura's face brightened. "Oh, I just hope mine is cute."

"Boys?" Dad asked. "What boys?"

I mentally kicked myself. I should have kept my mouth shut and surprised Laura when she walked down to the pool. Now I was going to have to explain things to my father.

"I met a boy today at Disney World," I said. "While you and Laura were in the special effects thing. I agreed to meet him and his friend at the pool this evening."

"You what?" Dad sounded shocked. "You invited strange boys to use our pool? This is private property."

"They live here," I explained. "And they're not strange."

I started to walk outside, but Dad held out his arm to stop me. "I am not happy about this, Brittany. I am not happy that you would speak to a boy you don't know, in a strange place, and then agree to meet him later. And I am especially unhappy you failed to mention this before now."

"Dad, he's a friend. Surely I'm allowed to make my own friends. I don't have to check my friends out with you, do I?"

"I am very upset," Dad said sternly. "In fact, I am not going to allow you to go to the pool unless you tell me more about this *friend*."

I sighed. "Dad, this is silly."

"I am serious, Brittany."

I sighed again. "Let's go to the pool. I think it'll be a big surprise."

"I've had enough of a surprise from your poor behavior," Dad scolded. "I certainly didn't expect this from you. Tell me more about this boy or you aren't going anywhere."

"You're going to spoil everything, Dad."

"Who is this boy?" Dad repeated.

Why did he have to be like this? How come he didn't know he was being unreasonable? Why was he wrecking Laura's surprise?

"Why can't you just chill out?" I shouted at him.

"I beg your pardon, Brittany." Little beads of sweat instantly appeared on his forehead.

"Chill out," I repeated. "Relax. Enjoy things. Stop being so uptight."

"Go to your room," he ordered.

"No," I said defiantly. "It's not my room. It's Sheila Whatever-her-name-is's guest room. And I'm not going there. You can punish me later if you want to. Right now,

I have to go meet my friend, Justin Adams."

"Justin Adams?" Dad's voice changed from anger to shock.

"Justin Adams?" Laura was more than a little shocked. "*The* Justin Adams?"

I nodded. "He was out for a break and . . . "

Laura didn't want to hear my story. She quickly twisted behind me, ducked under Dad's arm and charged toward the pool.

"Justin!" she yelled. "Justin! Justin!"

Chapter Fifteen

Sign My Face

When Dad and I reached the pool, we found Laura standing face-to-face with Justin, staring at him with wide eyes and a wide-open mouth. Justin stared back, looking a little afraid, almost as if he expected Laura to jump at him or bite him or worse.

"You're really him," Laura gushed. "You're really him." Then she turned to me. "You dirty, little . . . you tricked . . . you knew . . . no wonder you were glowing. Oh, Britt, thank you. And don't look so worried. I'm not going to say or do anything stupid. I learned my lesson this afternoon. I'm going to be just like you. Really sensible." She returned her attention to Justin. "Will you sign my arm?"

"This is my friend Laura," I said to

Justin. "We go to the same school in Toronto."

Justin reached out and shook her hand. "Nice to meet you, Laura."

As soon as he let go, Laura stared at her right palm. "He touched me. Justin Adams touched me."

"And this is my father," I continued with the introductions.

Justin shook hands with Dad. "Pleased to meet you, sir. I remember you from the studio this afternoon."

"The pleasure is mine," Dad replied. "I enjoyed the show very much, especially the plump rabbit."

"It's a living," Justin joked as he pointed at the pool. "That sea mammal in the water is Little Mike Davies. Both our families live in Los Angeles, but we board together with the same chaperone when we're filming in Florida."

Little Mike waved to us and we all waved back.

"Don't go too deep," Justin shouted. "Stay in the shallow end. You can't swim all that good yet."

"That's who the other boy was?" Laura guessed. "That's why you were being secretive, Britt?"

"Now I understand," Dad added. "I'm sorry I was being so awkward, Brittany. But your outburst was uncalled for. We are definitely going to talk later."

"Would everyone like some lemonade?" Justin offered. "I brought a pitcher and some tumblers down from the kitchen."

"I'd love some lemonade," Laura said. "Will you sign my arms and legs?"

"Do you want an autograph?" Justin asked.

Laura bobbed her head. "I want you to sign my face." She pointed at her cheek. "Right here. And . . ."

"Laura," I said as I tugged on my earring.

She seemed taken aback by my warning. "What? Am I saying stupid stuff?" She thought for a moment. "I guess I am. Just sign my arm."

"Your arm." Justin didn't sound too sure.

"Okay," Laura said. "How about my T-shirt?"

"Sure," Justin agreed. "Let's go sit down and get some lemonade and I'll be pleased to."

"You do that," Dad said. "I'm going back inside for a few minutes. I want to make a

127

phone call. Anyway, I'm sure you children don't really want me around to spoil your conversation."

Children. I gritted my teeth.

"Remember, I don't want you swimming in the deep end until I return," Dad warned.

"You only have to tell us once," I griped. "We got the message the first time."

Dad gave me the evil eye for a few seconds. "We'll talk later," he repeated. Then he turned around and walked back to the condo.

"Your father seems like a nice guy," Justin said as we sat around one of the pool-side tables.

"Sometimes," I complained. "If only I could get him to stop treating me like a three-year-old."

Justin poured lemonade for Laura and me. "Well, if I can figure how to make Sharon the Barbarian stop treating me the same way, I'll let you know how it's done." He nodded his head in the direction of one of the funny-shaped windows. "She's packing tonight or you'd see her head in that window every thirty seconds. Tonight, it's only every three minutes."

"At least she lets you go swimming alone. Laura and I can't even go in the deep end unless my father is watching."

"I'm a good swimmer," Justin said. "What can go wrong? I keep my eye on Little Mike."

"Exactly," I grumbled. "What can go wrong? How come my father can't understand that?"

"I don't have a pen," Laura moaned. "I don't have a pen so you can sign my shirt."

"There's lots in the apartment," Justin said. "We can do it later."

"I have your posters all over my room," Laura beamed. "You're so cute."

"Laura."

"That's not stupid, Britt," she said quickly. "That's the truth. I dream about you every night. If you were going to my school, I'd carry your books home. I'd do your homework. Anything."

"Laura."

Justin gave a nervous chuckle. "You sound like one of my fan letters."

"That's cause I probably wrote it," Laura explained. "I write to you three times a week. You keep sending me the same color photo and asking me to join your fan club. I've been a member for over six months. It's like you don't read what I write."

"To tell you the truth, the studio answers all my fan mail. They forward a few letters to me so I know what people are saying."

"You don't read my letters?" Laura sounded offended.

"I don't have the time . . . " Justin proceeded to tell her what he'd told me that afternoon. About his schedule, the tyranny of his chaperone and tutor and his lack of friends. " . . . and just sitting beside the pool with two girls is a special thrill for me."

"You hear what he said, Britt? He said *we're* a thrill. You don't think my hair is too curly or that I have too many freckles?"

"You look fine," he replied.

"Justin Adams just said I look *fine*." Laura sighed. "You don't mind my braces? I've been thinking maybe I should get pink ones when I get back to Toronto. Do you like pink braces?"

"Pink braces sounds great to me."

"Now that you approve, I'm definitely going to get pink ones," she concluded. "Could you say it to my face one time please? Pretty please?"

"Pardon?" It was obvious that Justin was as confused by Laura's conversation as I sometimes was. "Could I say what?"

"What you say every show. It's so sexy."

Justin looked at me and I shrugged in confusion.

"What are you talking about, Laura?" I asked.

"Your famous line," Laura explained. "You know, 'Do you want fries with that?' I melt every time you say that on TV."

"You do?" Justin said.

"Of course," Laura told him. "I dream about you walking up to me in the middle of Science class or in the middle of Gym and saying, 'Do you want fries with that?' It's my ultimate fantasy."

"It is?"

I wondered if I should be tugging on my earring.

"Please say it to me," Laura pleaded.

Justin agreed. "Okay, 'Do you want fries with that?' How's that?"

Laura did her fake faint.

"Is she okay?" Justin sounded a little worried.

Laura's eyes flipped open. "That's so cool. I can't believe you said 'Do you want fries with that?' to me."

"I . . . er . . . well . . . ." Justin looked majorly confused.

I figured it was time to change the subject. "I've been thinking about what you said this afternoon, Justin. You know, about us being friends. Well, I'd like to be your friend. And I'm sure Laura would, too."

"His friend? Would I like to be his friend. Is there any doubt? Oh, yes," Laura gushed. "Oh, yes. Definitely, yes."

Justin smiled. "That's great. You've made my day."

"You hear that, Britt," Laura squeaked. "We made his day. We made Justin Adams's day.

Justin cleared his throat. "Could I ask you guys to do me a favor? Now that we're friends."

"Anything," Laura said. "Who do we have to kill?"

Justin studied Laura again. "Pardon me?"

"That's Laura's idea of a joke," I told him. "She has a weird sense of humor."

She nodded. "Just a joke. What do you want us to do?"

"Please don't keep calling me Justin Adams. That's somebody else. That's the person who acts on *Do You Want Fries With That?* and he's not me. Would you call me by my real name?"

"That's not your real name?" Laura asked.

Justin shook his head. "Of course not. That's the name my agent thought up for me. She said it sounded more contemporary."

"Contemporary? What's that mean?" Laura asked.

"More 'today,'" I said.

"Oh." Laura leaned back in her chair, took a swallow of lemonade and asked the question for me. "What's your real name then?"

"Bob," Justin announced.

"Bob?" Laura said the name slowly. "Bob?"

"Bob is a nice name," I said.

"Bob?" Laura was still trying to get used to it. "Bob? What kind of name is Bob?"

I tugged at my earring.

"I mean, it's a nice name," Laura said diplomatically. "But it doesn't suit you."

"Is your name really Robert?" I asked.

"No, it's just Bob," he said. "My parents liked Bob. I'm Bob Bodnaruk."

"Justin Adams is Bob Bodnaruk?" Laura said in amazement. "I'm having lemonade with Bob Bodnaruk? I asked Bob Bodnaruk to sign my face? I have pictures of Bob Bodnaruk all over my bedroom? Bob Bodnaruk just said 'Do you want fries with that?' into my face? Somehow, it isn't quite the same."

"Sounds fine to me," I said. "I like it a lot, Bob." Truth was, I thought it sounded as strange as Laura did.

"Bob?" Laura babbled on.

I wished I had a sock to stick in her mouth.

"You should hear what Little Mike's real name is." Justin glanced over my shoulder. "Hey, Little Mike," he called. "Tell the girls what your real name is."

And then it happened.

Justin's face turned a sickly white color. It was as if the blood had retreated from his skin. His bottom lip shivered.

I twisted around and stared into the pool. Little Mike Davies was at the bottom of the deep end. His arms floated loosely at his sides.

He wasn't moving.

Chapter Sixteen

Seconds Count

I don't know what Laura said at that moment. It may have been more of a cry than words. But the fear in her voice reached inside me and squeezed my heart. A nauseating dullness spread through my guts.

And that made me move. I pushed my chair away and raced across the grass and patio stones. The water stung my face and chest as I plunged into the pool. Thrusting my arms in wide strokes, I forced myself down to the bottom of the deep end. My ears protested against the pressure. My eyes protested against the chlorine.

From somewhere in my head, I heard the voice of my swim instructor, Margo, from the Y in Toronto. I replayed her rescue class in my mind. "It's important to remember that seconds count," Margo said. "In an emergency, every second counts."

In my underwater vision, Little Mike was a blur with red hair. I grabbed for his arm and yanked him toward me, kicking my feet violently to get back to the surface. We moved slowly, as if we were swimming in syrup. My lungs began to ache, begging for breath.

Slowly, kick by kick, I tugged his lifeless body upward. Little Mike was too heavy. A five-year-old shouldn't weigh this much. That wasn't a good sign. It meant he was full of water.

I broke the surface, coughing and sputtering.

"Here," Justin called. "Over here."

I sucked in breath, coughed, and pulled Little Mike toward the outstretched arm at the side of the pool. Justin grabbed Mike by his hair and snatched him from my grasp. By the time I climbed out of the water, Justin had Mike lying on the patio stones.

"Laura's gone to get your father," Justin said. I noticed tears running down his face. "Why didn't I watch him all the time? I was only talking to you for a couple of minutes. Why didn't I watch him?"

A couple of minutes, I thought. Then I

heard Margo in my memory. "Every second counts. Every second counts."

I crawled over to Mike and watched his chest. He wasn't breathing.

"I'm wasting time," I said aloud. "I knew he wasn't breathing by the color of his face."

And I'm wasting time talking, I thought.

Little Mike's face was so blue. His lips were almost purple. I placed two fingers under his chin, rested my other hand on his forehead and gently tilted his head back.

"That's good, Britt," Margo coached in my mind. "Open the dummy's mouth. Check to see if there's anything in its mouth. If this was a real person, you'd be looking for food in the throat, or mucus, or false teeth. You might even be checking to see if the victim has swallowed his tongue."

Little Mike's mouth was full of water, I twisted his head slightly so it ran out.

"Pinch the nose," Margo's voice went on. "Pinch the nose so the air doesn't come out of the nostrils. We want the air to go into the lungs."

I straightened Little Mike's head and covered his mouth with mine. I exhaled. My breath brought another mouthful of water from Mike's throat. I twisted his head again.

"I should have watched him," Justin accused himself.

I was aware of someone running to my left.

"This is all my fault, Sharon," Justin moaned. "I should have been watching him."

"Oh, my Lord," a woman wailed.

I forced a lungful of air into Little Mike. His chest heaved.

"Good," Margo said in my mind. "That's the right way to do it, Britt. You'll get your rescue badge for sure."

Rescue badge, I thought. *This isn't for a stupid badge. This is the real thing. I'm trying to save a life. I hope I'm not too late. Don't let me be too late, God. Please.*

I forced another lungful into Little Mike. And another.

I felt a hand on my shoulder. "Brittany," my father said. "What are you . . . do you . . . ?"

I glanced up at him. "Leave me alone," I ordered. "I know what I'm doing."

"We called 9–1–1," Laura said from behind Dad.

Two more breaths. More water oozed from Little Mike's mouth. But he wasn't coughing it up himself. And he wasn't changing color. He was still blue.

"If you're doing it properly, you should note a change in color after four or five breaths," Margo lectured.

I am doing it properly, I thought. *His chest is moving. I'm bringing up water.*

I pressed two fingers against his neck to find his pulse. Nothing. His heart wasn't beating.

"His heart has stopped," I said out loud.

"Oh, my Lord," Sharon repeated.

Justin and Laura cried.

More legs joined us. The tenants of the condo formed a circle around me.

"Hurry up," Dad said. "Where's that ambulance?"

"Remember, with small children, you can't use both hands to simulate a heartbeat," Margo said in my head. "You might break ribs or cause internal damage. Place the heel of only one hand in the center of the chest, directly above where the breastbone ends."

I did as I'd been taught.

"Press down about two and a half to four centimeters, depending on the size of the child," Margo's voice continued. "Repeat for a total of five times."

I did. Then I gave Little Mike a deep breath. I checked his chest. He wasn't breathing on his own. I forced another breath into him.

Then I pumped his chest another five times. Followed by a breath. Five pumps on the chest. Breath. Five pumps. Breath. I checked his neck pulse again.

Still nothing.

"Can I do anything?" Dad asked.

"Do you know how to do CPR?" I asked quickly.

"No, but I could . . . ."

I shook my head. Margo lectured me again. "If you have an untrained person with you, it's best if you do not let them help. You can't afford to have them do the breathing incorrectly. And you should never let an untrained person help with external heart massage. The results could be deadly."

Five. One. Five. One. Five. One.

Little Mike's lips turned from purple to blue. His face lost the bluish tinge. Some of the freckles were returning.

I gently pushed my fingers into his neck again. This time I felt a heartbeat, fast and strong, a rapid *thadump, thadump, thadump*. But he still wasn't breathing on his own.

"Come on, Mike," I pleaded. "Breathe. Do it!"

"I hear a siren," Laura said. "Listen. I hear a siren."

I concentrated on forcing air into Mike's lungs.

"Breathe, you cute little twerp," Laura shouted.

In the middle of a breath, Little Mike's body shuddered in a violent spasm. He vomited water into my mouth, twisted his head on his own and began a series of gut-deep hacks. More water ran from his lips and nose.

"He's alive," Laura squeaked. "You did it, Britt. He's alive."

"Thank heavens," Sharon the chaperone wept.

I looked up to see her hugging Justin. He was still crying, but he was smiling too.

Dad knelt beside me. He placed a rolled-up towel under Mike's head and another towel to cover him.

"We need a blanket," Dad said. "Laura, run and get a blanket. Let's keep him warm."

I sat down on the patio stones and brushed my hand lightly through Little Mike's wet, red curls. His eyes were open, full of fear, looking up at me. "It's okay," I said softly. "It's going to be fine now. You feel like you're going to throw up some more?"

He shook his head, coughed a few more times and began to whimper. "That's okay," I told him. "There's an ambulance coming and . . . and everything is just all right."

I was sure it was. As Justin had said, it had only been a couple of minutes. Margo finished her lecture in my mind. "You have five to seven minutes to begin CPR after the heart stops. Any longer and the victim will suffer serious brain damage."

I couldn't be positive, of course, but just by the way Mike was looking up at me, I was pretty sure I'd been fast enough. It had only been a couple of minutes.

I don't remember what happened next all that well. I recall inching back when paramedics arrived. They checked Little Mike, did a few things to him. Somebody, I guess it was Laura, draped a blanket around my shoulders. All the people were talking, crying, even laughing in a relieved sort of way. Little Mike was placed on a stretcher. Justin and his chaperone followed the paramedics. Finally, the loud howl of the siren faded.

And then we were alone, Dad, Laura and me. My father and my best friend sat beside me on the patio stones. That struck me as a dumb thing to do. Why didn't they help me up so we could sit somewhere comfortable?

Laura took one of my hands and Dad took the other.

"You were terrific, Britt," Laura said. "You saved somebody's life."

"You *were* terrific," Dad agreed. He reached out to muss my hair and stopped. "You were . . . I never thought . . . you were so . . . ."

From deep inside me, from the place where the fear had clawed at whatever my insides were made of, came a shuddering sob. I grabbed my father, buried my face into his shoulder and cried.

Chapter Seventeen

Smiles

Little Mike is okay. The doctors said he suffered no permanent damage from the accident. In fact, the little guy bounced back so fast he was out of hospital the next day. By that time, his parents had joined him.

Little Mike's folks took us out for supper and thanked me with a gift. Little Mike's father works at Disneyland in California. He gave me an all-expense-paid trip to the west coast Disneyland for five people. I politely refused, of course, and told them it wasn't necessary. But they insisted. What could I do? I'm going to take Mom, her boyfriend Kevin, Laura and Bob Bodnaruk.

Justin — Bob — came over to our condo the morning after we'd saved Little Mike. He told us how great his co-star was doing. Then he said, "Sharon and I are leaving for the airport in a half hour. I'm going home and I wanted to say good-bye."

"You're going to call us, right?" Laura asked.

"You bet," Bob said. "After what happened last night, I figure we're good friends now."

"You hear that, Britt. We're *good* friends. That's sort of poetry, isn't it? Wait till the kids in Toronto hear this. Will you say it one more time please, Jus . . . I mean, Bob. Just say it one more time."

He made a wry smile. "Okay, here goes. 'Do you want fries with that?'"

"That's so romantic," Laura swooned. "I bet William Shakespeare must have written it. It's poetry."

Justin took a step closer to me. "Thank you, Britt." he said. "You were wonderful. You're the real superstar." And then Justin Adams leaned over and kissed me. It was just a peck, but it was on the lips.

"I hope that was the right thing to do," he said. "I kissed a girl in a *Do You Want Fries With That?* show once. That's how I thanked a girl who . . . "

"Rescued your dog," Laura finished. "When I saw that show, I wanted so much to be her. Say, do I get one too? You can kiss me. I ran for help. Remember? I helped call 9–1–1."

Justin nodded and kissed Laura on the cheek.

"Hey," she complained. "What's the problem? How come you kissed me on the cheek? Do you like Britt better?"

He didn't answer the question.

"We'll see you guys," he said.

I smiled. "We'll see you, Bob."

"I'll call you from LA," he promised.

And he did. That evening at Sheila's condo. That's when I told him Little Mike's parents had given me the trip, and invited him to join us.

Justin Adams said, "I've never been to Disneyland, even though I live here."

"I've never been to a Blue Jays game," I told him. "Or to the top of the CN Tower."

The next day we kept to our schedule and went to Epcot Center in Disney World. Like everything else, it was terrific. But I definitely wasn't *bubbly* excited. Things interested me, but I kept reliving what had happened in the pool. I think Dad did too. He didn't try to shuffle us around to make sure we were having fun.

Even Laura was subdued. The only weird thing she said in the morning was after we'd finished the Food Ride, which is a pretend ride through the human digestive system. "That was interesting," she observed. "I didn't know the inside of my body looked like that. It's a good job I don't have a window where my belly button is or I'd be sick to my stomach."

The rest of the morning she was sensible. Sensible for Laura anyway.

"I have to go to the bathroom," Laura informed us halfway through lunch. That left Dad and me alone at the table.

"I'm a little tired," Dad said. "Why don't you and Laura wander around by yourselves for a couple of hours this afternoon?"

I nearly choked on my burger. "Pardon? Laura and I? Go alone?"

"Sure," he nodded. "I've seen it all anyway. You girls could use some time by yourselves."

"Aren't you worried something might happen to us?"

"Yes," he said. "But then I figure, what can really happen to you here in the middle of all these people? Besides, you're a big girl now. I trust you won't get into trouble."

"But . . . ?"

He held up his hand to stop me. "Brittany, I haven't been fair to you this week.

You know, I worry about things. Maybe too much. I can't change that. That's just the way I am. I know you've felt angry about my concerns a couple of times this week."

"It's been frustrating, Dad," I confessed. "I've been trying to understand, but you've been so picky. I mean the earring bit, the make-up, and making me hold your hand."

"It seemed sensible to me," he defended. "And I still think twelve-year-olds shouldn't wear make up. But we're not discussing my opinions right now. We're dealing with how I should treat my daughter."

He stirred his coffee a few times as if he was searching for the right words. "Brittany, I care about you very much. Very much. But you have to understand I've never had a daughter growing up before. I see you once a year and I expect you to be the same as you were when we said good-bye twelve months ago."

"Fifteen."

He nodded. "A long time. I don't get to see you changing day by day."

"It would be nice if I could be with you more often," I said.

"I'm going to see to that. I'm going to make sure you visit me at least twice a year from now on. And I'm going to ask my boss if I can have part of the Ontario territory. No promises, but maybe I can spend some time in Toronto each year."

"That would be great."

"Anyway, Brittany, what I'm trying to say is that you've always been my little girl. When I met you at the airport the other day, I noticed how much you'd changed. And I didn't know how to handle it. So I treated you the same way I always had."

"Laura told me her father was the same way," I said.

"Well, I'm glad I'm not the only one," Dad went on. "When I watched you last night saving Little Mike's life, I realized my daughter wasn't the little girl I once knew. I'm sorry I was being so . . . "

" . . . overprotective?"

He bit his bottom lip. "I guess that's the right word. I'll try to treat you more like a young woman." Then he quickly added. "But not too much like a young woman. You *are* only twelve."

"I'm nearly thirteen."

He just smiled at me.

"You won't muss my hair anymore?" I requested.

"Agreed," he said. "And I promise to

listen to your complaints from now on."

"You know, Dad, I didn't act all that mature this week. Laura suggested I should talk to you and I didn't listen. I held it inside and got frustrated and angry."

"I wouldn't have listened anyway," he said. "I guess, in a way, it was me who was being childish. But that's changed now."

Then he reached across the table and squeezed my hands. "I called Sheila this morning. Like I said, she's in Chicago on business, but she's going to cancel everything for the rest of the week. She's coming back to her condo tonight. I want you to meet her. She wants to meet you. We like each other very much."

I winked. "Sounds serious. I'm sure I'll like her."

* * * * *

Dad and I were almost finished eating when Laura returned.

"You were gone for a long time," Dad noted.

"I had to go to the bathroom," she said. "Sometimes it takes time. And I had to brush my hair." Then she started chuckling. "Want to hear something funny?"

"About the bathroom?" I asked suspiciously.

"No," she said. "About hair. When I was little, I saw my mother spraying her hair, so I decided I was going to do it too. I went to the cupboard and got a can. Of course, I was too young to read and I didn't know I'd grabbed a can of bug killer. I sprayed my head with Raid. Can you believe that?"

"Yes," Dad answered seriously.

"My mom says flies landed on my head and dropped dead, but I think she was just joking."

My father nodded.

"Then there was the time I brushed my teeth with sun screen," Laura continued. "And another time, I poured fabric softener in the tub because I thought it was bubble bath. My skin was really smooth when I got out. Can you imagine me doing something so weird, Mr. P?"

"Yes, I can, Laura."

"Say, Mr. P, speaking of hair, I've noticed you're getting a little thin on top. You bothered by that?"

I pulled on an earring, figuring Dad would be embarrassed. To my surprise, he wasn't upset.

"Not at all," Dad answered. "A receding hairline is simply part of the male maturation process."

"Huh?" Laura grunted.

"It doesn't bother me," my father explained. "It's part of growing older."

"Oh." Laura nodded. "I understand. Like getting a shape?"

My father took a bite of hamburger so he wouldn't have to answer.

Laura was still on a roll. "My Uncle Mortie lives in Winnipeg and he's bald and he hates it. When I was a kid he visited us and he'd sprayed his head with this stuff that looks like hair. This is real stuff, Mr. P. It comes in a can and when you spray it on your head it looks like real hair. I've seen it in those infomercial things on TV."

Dad swallowed. "I've seen it advertised too."

"Anyway, when Uncle Mortie was visiting, I was watering the flowers in the back yard with the hose. Uncle Mortie snuck up beside me, shouted 'Boo!' and scared me so much I dropped the hose. It started snaking on the ground. Uncle Mortie and I got soaked."

"Must have been funny," I said.

"Funnier was when the water hit the hair stuff on Uncle Mortie's head. It melted it. Clumps of black goo dripped down his face. He looked like something from a horror movie. I didn't have a clue what was going on so I ran into the house screaming, 'It's melting! Uncle Mortie's head is melting!'"

Laura shouted the last sentence and everyone in the restaurant stopped eating and turned to look at her. Laura noticed and smiled at the crowd. "It's okay," she said in a loud voice. "It wasn't his head. It was just his hair. Only his hair melted."

I laughed. I pictured these people returning home and telling their friends about the girl in the restaurant with the melting head.

Dad stared at us as if he couldn't believe Laura and I were really friends. Then his expression dissolved into a warm grin. "You are a different young woman," Dad said. "I mean that as a compliment."

"Hey," Laura grinned back. "What can I say?"

"Well, I guess I'll be on my way. Have you girls had enough to eat?" Dad asked.

"I'm still a little hungry, Mr. P," Laura answered. "I think I'm going to get another burger."

"Hey, Laura," I said.

"What, Britt?"

"Do you want fries with that?"

Of course, we laughed at that too.

MARTYN GODFREY is the author of more than two dozen books for young people, including the JAWS Mob series, the Ms Teeny-Wonderful series, *Why Just Me?* and *I Spent My Summer Vacation Kidnapped into Space*. His novel *Mystery in the Frozen Lands* won the Geoffrey Bilson Award for Historical Fiction for Young People.

Martyn wrote his first story when he was a junior high school teacher, on a challenge from a student. That story became his first book: *The Day the Sky Exploded*. Now Martyn writes full-time. His home base is in Edmonton, Alberta, but he spends much of his time travelling around the country talking to kids about books and writing.